THE
RAT-CATCHER'S
DAUGHTER

THE
RAT-CATCHER'S
DAUGHTER

A Collection of Stories by

LAURENCE HOUSMAN

Selected and with an afterword by

ELLIN GREENE

Illustrated by Julia Noonan

A Margaret K. McElderry Book

ATHENEUM   1974   NEW YORK

"Rocking-Horse Land," "Gammelyn, the Dress-maker," "The Prince with the Nine Sorrows," "The White Doe," "A Chinese Fairy Tale," "Happy Returns" taken from *Moonshine and Clover;* "The Rat-Catcher's Daughter," "The Traveller's Shoes," "The Wooing of the Maze," "Koonie in the Sleeping Palace" taken from *A Doorway in Fairyland;* "The Cloak of Friendship" taken from *All-Fellows and the Cloak of Friendship;* "Moozipoo" taken from *What O'Clock Tales.*

J
H

For Dorothy May

Contents

———— ◆ ————

ONE

The Rat-Catcher's Daughter

O nce upon a time there lived an old rat-catcher who had a daughter, the most beautiful girl that had ever been born. Their home was a dirty little cabin; but they were not so poor as they seemed, for every night the rat-catcher took the rats he had cleared out of one house and let them go at the door of another, so that on the morrow he might be sure of a fresh job.

His rats got quite to know him and would run to him when he called; people thought him the most wonderful rat-catcher and could not make out how it was that a rat remained within reach of his operations.

Now anyone can see that a man who practiced so cunning a roguery was greedy beyond the intentions of Providence. Every day, as he watched his daughter's

beauty increase, his thoughts were: "When will she be able to pay me back for all the expense she has been to me?" He would have grudged her the very food she ate, if it had not been necessary to keep her in the good looks, which were some day to bring him his fortune. For he was greedier than any gnome after gold.

Now all good gnomes have this about them: they love whatever is beautiful and hate to see harm happen to it. A gnome who lived far away underground below where stood the rat-catcher's house, said to his fellows: "Up yonder is a man who has a daughter; so greedy is he, he would sell her to the first comer who gave him gold enough! I am going up to look after her."

So one night, when the rat-catcher set a trap, the gnome went and got himself caught in it. There in the morning, when the rat-catcher came, he found a funny little fellow, all bright and golden, wriggling and beating to be free.

"I can't get out!" cried the little gnome. "Let me go!"

The rat-catcher screwed up his mouth to look virtuous. "If I let you out, what will you give me?"

"A sack full of gold," answered the gnome, "just as heavy as myself—not a pennyweight less!"

"Not enough!" said the rat-catcher. "Guess again!"

"As heavy as you are!" cried the gnome, beginning to plead in a thin, whining tone.

"I'm a poor man," said the rat-catcher; "a poor man mayn't afford to be generous!"

"What is it you want of me?" cried the gnome.

"If I let you go," said the rat-catcher, "you must make me the richest man in the world!" Then he thought of his daughter: "Also you must make the king's son marry my daughter; then I will let you go."

The gnome laughed to himself to see how the trapper was being trapped in his own avarice as, with the most melancholy air, he answered: "I can make you the richest man in the world; but I know of no way of making the king's son marry your daughter, except one."

"What way?" asked the rat-catcher.

"Why," answered the gnome, "for three years your daughter must come and live with me underground, and by the end of the third year her skin will be changed into pure gold like ours. And do you know any king's son who would refuse to marry a beautiful maiden who was pure gold from the sole of her foot to the crown of her head?"

The rat-catcher had so greedy an inside that he could not believe in any king's son refusing to marry a maiden of pure gold. So he clapped hands on the bargain and let the gnome go.

The gnome went down into the ground and fetched up sacks and sacks of gold, until he had made the rat-catcher the richest man in the world. Then the father called his daughter, whose name was Jasomé, and bade her follow the gnome down into the heart of the earth.

It was all in vain that Jasomé begged and implored; the rat-catcher was bent on having her married to the king's son. So he pushed, and the gnome pulled, and

down she went; and the earth closed after her.

The gnome brought her down to his home under the hill upon which stood the town. Everywhere round her were gold and precious stones; the very air was full of gold dust, so that when she remained still it settled on her hands and her hair, and a soft golden down began to show itself over her skin. So there in the house of the gnome sat Jasomé and cried; and, far away over-head, she heard the days come and go by the sound of people walking and the rolling of wheels.

The gnome was very kind to her; nothing did he spare of underground commodities that might afford her pleasure. He taught her the legends of all the heroes that have gone down into earth and been forgotten, and the lost songs of the old poets, and the buried languages that once gave wisdom to the world: down there all these things are remembered.

She became the most curiously accomplished and wise maiden that ever was hidden from the light of day. "I have to train you," said the gnome, "to be fit for a king's bride!" But Jasomé, though she thanked him, only cried to be let out.

In front of the rat-catcher's house rose a little spring of salt water with gold dust in it, that gilded the basin where it sprang. When he saw it, he began rubbing his hands with delight, for he guessed well enough that his daughter's tears had made it; and the dust in it told him how surely now she was being turned into gold.

And now the rat-catcher was the richest man in the

world: all his traps were made of gold, and when he went rat-hunting he rode in a gilded coach drawn by twelve hundred of the finest and largest rats. This was for an advertisement of the business. He now caught rats for the fun of it and the show of it, but also to get money by it; for, though he was so rich, ratting and money-grubbing had become a second nature to him; unless he were at one or the other, he could not be happy.

Far below, in the house of the gnome, Jasomé sat and cried. When the sound of the great bells ringing for Easter came down to her, the gnome said: "Today I cannot bind you; it is the great rising day for all Christians. If you wish, you may go up and ask your father now to release you."

So Jasomé kissed the gnome and went up the track of her own tears that brought her to her father's door. When she came to the light of day, she felt quite blind; a soft yellow tint was all over her, and already her hair was quite golden.

The rat-catcher was furious when he saw her coming back before her time. "Oh, father," she cried, "let me come back for a little while to play in the sun!" But her father, fearing lest the gilding of her complexion should be spoiled, drove her back into the earth and trampled it down over her head.

The gnome seemed quite sorry for her when she returned; but already, he said, a year was gone—and what were three years when a king's son would be the reward?

At the next Easter he let her go again; and now she looked quite golden, except for her eyes and her white teeth and the nails on her pretty little fingers and toes. But again her father drove her back into the ground and put a heavy stone slab over the spot to make sure of her.

At last the third Easter came, and she was all gold.

She kissed the gnome many times and was almost sorry to leave him, for he had been very kind to her. And now he told her about her father catching him in the trap, and robbing him of his gold by a hard bargain, and of his being forced to take her down to live with him till she was turned into gold, so that she might marry the king's son. "For now," said he, "you are so compounded of gold that only the gnomes could rub it off you."

So this time, when Jasomé came up once more to the light of day, she did not go back again to her cruel father but went and sat by the roadside and played with the sunbeams and wondered when the king's son would come and marry her.

And as she sat there all the country people who passed by stopped and mocked her; and boys came and threw mud at her because she was all gold from head to foot —an object, to be sure, for all simple folk to laugh at. So presently, instead of hoping, she fell to despair and sat weeping with her face hidden in her hands.

Before long the king's son came that road and saw something shining like sunlight on a pond; but when he came near, he found a lovely maiden of pure gold lying

in a pool of her own tears with her face hidden in her hair.

Now the king's son, unlike the country folk, knew the value of gold; but he was grieved at heart for a maiden so stained all over with it, and more, when he beheld how she wept. So he went to lift her up; and there, surely, he saw the most beautiful face he could ever have dreamed of. But, alas! so discolored—even her eyes, and her lips, and the very tears she shed were the color of gold! When he could bring her to speak, she told him how, because she was all gold, all the people mocked at her and boys threw mud at her; and she had nowhere to go, unless it were back to the kind gnome who lived underground, out of sight of the sweet sun.

So the prince said, "Come with me, and I will take you to my father's palace, and there nobody shall mock you, but you shall sit all your days in the sunshine and be happy."

And as they went, more and more he wondered at her great beauty—so spoiled that he could not look at her without grief—and was taken with increasing wonder at the beautiful wisdom stored in her golden mind; for she told him the tales of the heroes, which she had learned from the gnome, and of buried cities; also the songs of old poets that have been forgotten; and her voice, like the rest of her, was golden.

The prince said to himself, "I shut my eyes and am ready to die loving her; yet, when I open them, she is but a talking statue!"

One day he said to her, "Under all this disguise you must be the most beautiful thing upon earth! Already to me you are the dearest!" and he sighed, for he knew that a king's son might not marry a figure of gold.

Now one day after this, as Jasomé sat alone in the sunshine and cried, the little old gnome stood before her and said, "Well, Jasomé, have you married the king's son?"

"Alas!" cried Jasomé, "you have so changed me: I am no longer human! Yet he loves me, and, but for that, he would marry me."

"Dear me!" said the gnome. "If that is all, I can take the gold off of you again: why, I said so!"

Jasomé entreated him, by all his former kindness, to do so for her now.

"Yes," said the gnome, "but a bargain is a bargain. Now is the time for me to get back my bags of gold. Do you go to your father and let him know that the king's son is willing to marry you if he restores to me my treasure that he took from me; for that is what it comes to."

Up jumped Jasomé and ran to the rat-catcher's house. "Oh, father," she cried, "now you can undo all your cruelty to me; for now, if you will give back the gnome his gold, he will give my own face back to me, and I shall marry the king's son!"

But the rat-catcher was filled with admiration at the sight of her and would not believe a word she said. "I have given you your dowry," he answered; "three years I had to do without you to get it. Take it away, and

get married, and leave me the peace and plenty I have so hardly earned!"

Jasomé went back and told the gnome. "Really," said he, "I must show this rat-catcher that there are other sorts of traps and that it isn't only rats and gnomes that get caught in them! I have given him his taste of wealth; now it shall act as pickle to his poverty!"

So the next time the rat-catcher put his foot out of doors, the ground gave way under it and—snap!— the gnome had him by the leg.

"Let me go!" cried the rat-catcher; "I can't get out!"

"Can't you?" said the gnome. "If I let you out, what will you give me?"

"My daughter!" cried the rat-catcher; "my beautiful golden daughter!"

"Oh, no!" laughed the gnome. "Guess again!"

"My own weight in gold!" cried the rat-catcher, in a frenzy; but the gnome would not close the bargain till he had wrung from the rat-catcher the promise of his last penny.

So the gnome carried away all the sacks of gold before the rat-catcher's eyes; and when he had them safe underground, then at last he let the old man go. Then he called Jasomé to follow him, and she went down willingly into the black earth.

For a whole year the gnome rubbed and scrubbed and tubbed her to get the gold out of her composition; and when it was done, she was the most shiningly beautiful thing you ever set eyes on.

When she got back to the palace, she found her

dear prince pining for love of her, and wondering when she would return. So they were married the very next day; and the rat-catcher came to look on at the wedding.

He grumbled because he was in rags and because he was poor; he wept that he had been robbed of his money and his daughter. But gnomes and daughters, he said, were in one and the same box; such ingratitude as theirs no one could beat.

TWO

—◆—

Rocking-Horse Land

Little Prince Freedling woke up with a jump and sprang out of bed into the sunshine. He was five years old that morning by all the clocks and calendars in the kingdom; and the day was going to be beautiful. Every golden minute was precious. He was dressed and out of his room before the attendants knew that he was awake.

In the antechamber stood piles on piles of glittering presents; when he walked among them they came up to the measure of his waist. His fairy godmother had sent him a toy with the most humorous effect. It was labeled, "Break me and I shall turn into something else." So every time he broke it, he got a new toy more beautiful than the last. It began by being a hoop, and from that it ran on, while the Prince broke it incessantly for the space of one hour, during which it became by

turns—a top, a Noah's ark, a skipping rope, a man-of-war, a box of bricks, a picture puzzle, a pair of stilts, a drum, a trumpet, a kaleidoscope, a steam engine, and nine hundred and fifty other things exactly. Then he began to grow discontented, because it would never turn into the same thing again; and after having broken the man-of-war, he wanted to get it back again. Also he wanted to see if the steam engine would go inside the Noah's ark; but the toy would never be two things at the same time either. This was very unsatisfactory. He thought his fairy godmother ought to have sent him two toys, out of which he could make combinations.

At last he broke it once more, and it turned into a kite; and while he was flying the kite he broke the string, and the kite went sailing away up into nasty blue sky and was never heard of again.

Then Prince Freedling sat down and howled at his fairy godmother; what a dissembling lot fairy god-mothers were, to be sure! They were always setting traps to make their godchildren unhappy. Nevertheless, when told to, he took up his pen and wrote her a nice little note, full of bad spelling and tarradiddles, to say what a happy birthday he was spending in breaking up the beautiful toy she had sent him.

Then he went to look at the rest of the presents and found it quite refreshing to break a few that did not send him giddy by turning into anything else.

Suddenly his eyes became fixed with delight; alone, right at the end of the room, stood a great black rocking-horse. The saddle and bridle were hung with tiny gold

bells and balls of coral; and the horse's tail and mane flowed till they almost touched the ground.

The Prince scampered across the room and threw his arms around the beautiful creature's neck. All its bells jangled as the head swayed gracefully down; and the prince kissed it between the eyes. Great eyes they were, the color of fire, so wonderfully bright, it seemed they must be really alive, only they did not move, but gazed continually with a set stare at the tapestry-hung wall, on which were figures of armed knights riding to battle.

So Prince Freedling mounted to the back of his rocking-horse; and all day long he rode and shouted to the figures of the armed knights, challenging them to fight, or leading them against the enemy.

At length, when it came to be bedtime, weary of so much glory, he was lifted down from the saddle and carried away to bed.

In his sleep Freedling still felt his black rocking-horse swinging to and fro under him and heard the melodious chime of its bells and, in the land of dreams, saw a great country open before him, full of the sound of the battle cry and the hunting horn calling him to strange perils and triumphs.

In the middle of the night he grew softly awake, and his heart was full of love for his black rocking-horse. He crept gently out of bed: he would go and look at it where it was standing so grand and still in the next room, to make sure that it was all safe and not afraid of being by itself in the dark night. Parting the

door hangings he passed through into the wide hollow chamber beyond, all littered about with toys.

The moon was shining in through the window, making a square cistern of light upon the floor. And then, all at once, he saw that the rocking-horse had moved from the place where he had left it! It had crossed the room and was standing close to the window with its head toward the night, as though watching the movement of the clouds and the trees swaying in the wind.

The Prince could not understand how it had been moved so; he was a little bit afraid, and stealing timidly across, he took hold of the bridle to comfort himself with the jangle of its bells. As he came close and looked up into the dark solemn face, he saw that the eyes were full of tears and, reaching up, felt one fall warm against his hand.

"Why do you weep, my Beautiful?" said the Prince.

The rocking-horse answered, "I weep because I am a prisoner and not free. Open the window, Master, and let me go!"

"But if I let you go, I shall lose you," said the Prince. "Cannot you be happy here with me!"

"Let me go," said the horse, "for my brothers call me out of Rocking-Horse Land; I hear my mare whinnying to her foals; and they all cry, seeking me through the ups and hollows of my native fastnesses! Sweet Master, let me go this night, and I will return to you when it is day!"

Then Freedling said, "How shall I know that you will return: and what name shall I call you by?"

And the rocking-horse answered, "My name is Rollonde. Search my mane till you find in it a white hair; draw it out and wind it upon one of your fingers; and so long as you have it so wound, you are my master; and wherever I am, I must return at your bidding."

So the Prince drew down the rocking-horse's head, and searching the mane, he found the white hair and wound it upon his finger and tied it. Then he kissed Rollonde between the eyes, saying, "Go, Rollonde, since I love you and wish you to be happy; only return to me when it is day!" And so saying, he threw open the window to the stir of the night.

Then the rocking-horse lifted his dark head and neighed aloud for joy, and swaying forward with a mighty circling motion rose full into the air and sprang out into the free world before him.

Freedling watched how with plunge and curve he went over the bowed trees; and again he neighed into the darkness of the night, then swifter than wind disappeared in the distance. And faintly from far away came a sound of the neighing of many horses answering him.

Then the Prince closed the window and crept back to bed; and all night long he dreamed strange dreams of Rocking-Horse Land. There he saw smooth hills and valleys that rose and sank without a stone or a tree to disturb the steellike polish of their surface, slippery as glass, and driven over by a strong wind; and over them, with a sound like the humming of bees, flew the rocking-horses. Up and down, up and down, with bright manes

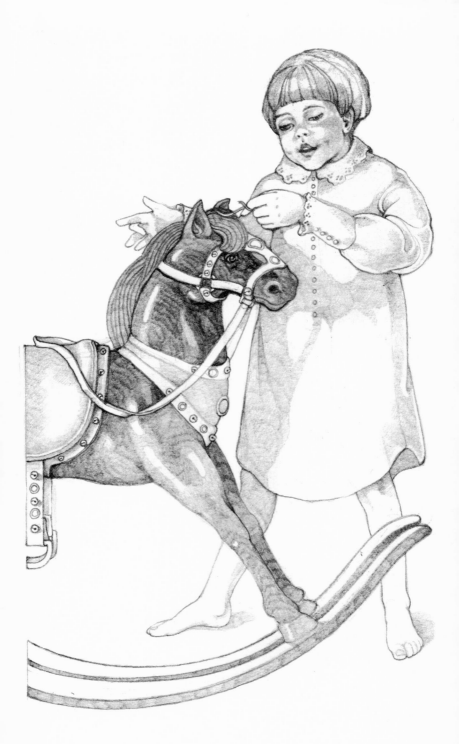

streaming like colored fires and feet motionless behind and before, went the swift pendulum of their flight. Their long bodies bowed and rose; their heads worked to give impetus to their going; they cried, neighing to each other over hill and valley, "Which of us shall be first? which of us shall be first?" After them the mares with their tall foals came spinning to watch, crying also among themselves, "Ah! which shall be first?"

"Rollonde, Rollonde is first!" shouted the Prince, clapping his hands as they reached the goal; and at that, all at once, he woke and saw it was broad day. Then he ran and threw open the window, and holding out the finger that carried the white hair, cried, "Rollonde, Rollonde, come back, Rollonde!"

Far away he heard an answering sound; and in another moment there came the great rocking-horse himself, dipping and dancing over the hills. He crossed the woods and cleared the palace wall at a bound, and floating in through the window, dropped to rest at Prince Freedling's side, rocking gently to and fro as though panting from the strain of his long flight.

"Now are you happy?" asked the Prince as he caressed him.

"Ah! sweet Prince," said Rollonde, "ah, kind Master!" And then he said no more, but became the stock-still staring rocking-horse of the day before, with fixed eyes and rigid limbs, which could do nothing but rock up and down with a jangling of sweet bells so long as the Prince rode him.

That night Freedling came again when all was still

in the palace; and now as before Rollonde had moved from his place and was standing with his head against the window waiting to be let out. "Ah, dear Master," he said, so soon as he saw the Prince coming, "let me go this night also, and surely I will return with day."

So again the Prince opened the window and watched him disappear and heard from far away the neighing of the horses in Rocking-Horse Land calling to him. And in the morning with the white hair round his finger he called, "Rollonde, Rollonde!" and Rollonde neighed and came back to him, dipping and dancing over the hills.

Now this same thing happened every night; and every morning the horse kissed Freedling, saying, "Ah! dear Prince and kind Master," and became stock-still once more.

So a year went by, till one morning Freedling woke up to find it was his sixth birthday. And as six is to five, so were the presents he received on his sixth birthday for magnificence and multitude to the presents he had received the year before. His fairy godmother had sent him a bird, a real live bird; but when he pulled its tail it became a lizard, and when he pulled the lizard's tail, it became a mouse, and when he pulled the mouse's tail, it became a cat. Then he did very much want to see if the cat would eat the mouse, and not being able to have them both he got rather vexed with his fairy godmother. However, he pulled the cat's tail, and the cat became a dog, and when he pulled the dog's, the dog became a goat; and so it went on till he got to a cow.

And he pulled the cow's tail and it became a camel, and he pulled the camel's tail and it became an elephant, and still not being contented, he pulled the elephant's tail and it became a guinea pig. Now a guinea pig has no tail to pull, so it remained a guinea pig, while Prince Freedling sat down and howled at his fairy godmother.

But the best of all his presents was the one given to him by the King his father. It was a most beautiful horse, for, said the King, "You are now old enough to learn to ride."

So Freedling was put upon the horse's back, and from having ridden so long upon his rocking-horse he learned to ride perfectly in a single day and was declared by all the courtiers to be the most perfect equestrian that was ever seen.

Now these praises and the pleasure of riding a real horse so occupied his thoughts that that night he forgot all about Rollonde, and falling fast asleep, dreamed of nothing but real horses and horsemen going to battle. And so it was the next night too.

But the night after that, just as he was falling asleep, he heard someone sobbing by his bed, and a voice saying, "Ah! dear Prince and kind Master, let me go, for my heart breaks for a sight of my native land." And there stood his poor rocking-horse Rollonde, with tears falling out of his beautiful eyes onto the white coverlet.

Then the Prince, full of shame at having forgotten his friend, sprang up and threw his arms round his neck saying, "Be of good cheer, Rollonde, for now surely I will let thee go!" and he ran to the window

and opened it for the horse to go through. "Ah, dear Prince and kind Master!" said Rollonde. Then he lifted his head and neighed so that the whole palace shook, and swaying forward till his head almost touched the ground, he sprang out into the night and away toward Rocking-Horse Land.

Then Prince Freedling, standing by the window, thoughtfully unloosed the white hair from his finger and let it float into the darkness, out of sight of his eye or reach of his hand.

"Good-bye, Rollonde," he murmured softly, "brave Rollonde, my own good Rollonde! Go and be happy in your own land, since I, your Master, was forgetting to be kind to you." And far away he heard the neighing of horses in Rocking-Horse Land.

Many years after, when Freedling had become King in his father's stead, the fifth birthday of the Prince his son came to be celebrated; and there on the morning of the day, among all the presents that covered the floor of the chamber, stood a beautiful foal rocking-horse, black, with deep-burning eyes.

No one knew how it had come there or whose present it was, till the King himself came to look at it. And when he saw it so like the old Rollonde he had loved as a boy, he smiled and, stroking its dark mane, said softly in its ear, "Art thou, then, the son of Rollonde?" And the foal answered him, "Ah, dear Prince and kind Master!" but never a word more.

Then the King took the little Prince his son and told him the story of Rollonde as I have told it here;

and at the end he went and searched in the foal's mane till he found one white hair, and drawing it out, he wound it about the little Prince's finger, bidding him guard it well and be ever a kind master to Rollonde's son.

So here is my story of Rollonde come to a good ending.

——— ◆·◆ ———

THREE

Gammelyn, the Dressmaker

There was once upon a time a King's daughter who was about to be given in marriage to a great prince; and when the wedding day was yet a long way off, the whole court began to concern itself as to how the bride was to be dressed. What she should wear and how she should wear it was the question debated by the King and his Court day and night, almost without interruption. Whatever it was to be, it must be splendid, without peer. Must it be silk, or velvet, or satin; should it be enriched with brocade or with gems or sewn thick with pearls?

But when they came to ask the Princess, she said, "I will have only a dress of beaten gold, light as gossamer, thin as beeswing, soft as swansdown."

Then the King, calling his chief goldsmith, told him

to make for the Princess the dress of beaten gold. But the goldsmith knew no way how such a dress was to be made, and his answer to the King was, "Sire, the thing is not to be done."

Then the King grew very angry, for he said, "What a Princess can find it in her head to wish, some man must find it in his wits to accomplish." So he put the chief goldsmith in prison to think about it and, summoning all the goldsmiths in the kingdom, told them of the Princess's wish, that a dress should be made for her of beaten gold. But every one of the goldsmiths went down on his knees to the King, saying, "Sire, the thing is not to be done." Thereupon the King clapped them all into prison, promising to cut off all their heads if in three weeks' time they had not put them together to some purpose and devised a plan for making such a dress as the Princess desired.

Now just then Gammelyn was passing through the country, and when he heard of all this, he felt very sorry for the goldsmiths, who had done nothing wrong, but had told honest truth about themselves to the King. So he set his bright wits to work, and at last said, "I think I can save the goldsmiths their heads for I have found a way of making such a dress as this fine Princess desires."

Then he went to the King and said, "I have a way for making a dress of beaten gold."

"But," said the King, "have a care, for if you fail I shall assuredly cut off your head."

All the same Gammelyn took that risk willingly and

set to work. And first he asked that the Princess would tell him what style of dress it should be; and the Princess said, "Beaten gold, light as gossamer, thin as beeswing, soft as swansdown, and it must be made thus." So she showed him of what fashion sleeve and bodice and train should be. Then Gammelyn caused to be made (for he had a palace full of workers put under him) a most lovely dress, in the fashion the Princess had named, of white cambric closely woven; and the Princess came wondering at him, saying that it was to be only of beaten gold.

"You wait awhile!" said Gammelyn, for he had no liking for the Princess. Then he asked the King for gold out of his treasury; but the King supplied him instead with gold from the stores of the imprisoned goldsmiths. So he put it in a sack and carried it to a mill and said to the miller, "Grind me this sack full of gold into flour." At first the miller stared at him for a madman, but when he saw the letter in Gammelyn's hands, which the King had written, and which said, "I'll cut off your head if you don't!" then he set to with a will and ground the gold into fine golden flour. So Gammelyn shouldered his sack and jogged back to the palace. The next thing he did was to summon all the goldbeaters in the kingdom, which he did easily enough with the King's letter; for directly they saw the words "I'll cut off your head if you don't!" and the King's signature beneath, they came running as fast as their legs could carry them, till all the streets which led up to the palace were full of them.

Then Gammelyn chose a hundred of the strongest and took them into the chamber where the wedding dress was in making. And the dress he took and spread out on iron tables and, sprinkling the golden flour all over it, set the men to beat day and night for a whole week. And at the end of the week there was a splendid dress that looked as if it were of pure gold only. But the Princess said, "My dress must be *all* gold, and no part cambric—this will not do." "You wait!" said Gammelyn, "it is not finished yet."

Then he made a fire of sweet spices and sandalwood, jasmine, and mignonette; and into the fire he put the wonderful dress.

The Princess screamed with grief and rage; for she was in love with the dress, though she was so nice in holding him to the conditions of the decree. But Gammelyn persevered, and what happened was this: the fire burnt away all the threads of the cambric, but was not hot enough to melt the gold; and when all the cambric was burnt, then he drew out of the fire a dress of beaten gold, light as gossamer, thin as bee's-wing, soft as swan's-down, and fragrant as a wind when it blows through a Sultan's garden.

So all the goldsmiths were set free from prison; and the King appointed Gammelyn his chief goldsmith.

But when the Princess saw the dress, she was so beside herself with pride and pleasure that she must have also a dress made of pearl, light as gossamer, thin as beeswing, soft as swansdown. And the King sent for all his jewelers and told them that such a dress

was to be made; but they all went down on their bended knees, crying with one voice, "Sire, the thing is not to be done." And all the good they got for that was that they were clapped into prison till a way for doing it should be found.

Then the King said to Gammelyn, "Since my jewelers cannot make this dress, you must do it!" But Gammelyn said, "Sire, that is not in our bargain." And the only answer the King had to that was, "I'll cut off your head if you don't."

Gammelyn sighed like a seashell; but determining to make the best of a bad business, he set to work.

And, as before, he made a dress in the fashion the Princess chose, of the finest weaving. He made each part separate; the two sleeves separate, the body separate, the skirt and train separate. Then, at his desire, the King commanded that all the oysters, which were dredged out of the sea, should be brought to him. Out of these he selected the five finest oysters of all; each one was the size of a tea tray. Then he put them into a large tank, and inside each shell he put one part of the dress—the weaving of which was so fine that there was plenty of room for it, as well as for the oysters. And in course of time he drew out from each shell—from one the body, from one the skirt, from one the train, from one a sleeve, from another the other sleeve. Next he fastened each part together with thread, and put the whole dress back into the tank; and into the mouth of one oyster he put the joinery of body and skirt, and

into the mouth of another the joinery of skirt and train, and into the mouth of two others the joinery of the two sleeves, and the fifth oyster he ate. So the oysters did their work, laying their soft inlay over the gown, just as they laid it over the inside of their shells; and after a time Gammelyn drew forth a dress bright and gleaming, and pure mother-of-pearl. But "No," said the Princess, "it must be all pure pearl, with nothing of thread in it." But, "Wait awhile!" said Gammelyn, "I have not finished yet."

So by a decree of the King he caused to be gathered together all the moths in the kingdom—millions of moths; and he put them all into a bare iron room along with the dress and sealed the doors and windows with red sealing wax. The Princess wept and sighed for the dress: "It will be all eaten," said she. "Then I shall cut off his head," said the King. But for all that, Gammelyn persevered.

And when he opened the door, they found that every thread had been eaten away by the moths, while the mother-of-pearl had been left uninjured. So the dress was a perfect pearl, light as gossamer, thin as bees-wing, soft as swansdown; and the King made Gammelyn his chief jeweler and set all the other jewelers free.

Then the Princess was so delighted that she wished to have one more dress also, made all of butterflies' wings. "That were easily done," said Gammelyn, "but it were cruel to ask for such a dress to be made."

Nevertheless the Princess would have it so, and *he* should make it. "I'll cut off your head if you don't," said the King.

Gammelyn bumbled like a bee; but all he said was, "Many million butterflies will be wanted for such a work: you must let me have again the two dresses—the pearl, and the gold—for butterflies love bright colors that gleam and shine; and with these alone can I gather them all to one place."

So the Princess gave him the two dresses; and he went to the highest part of the palace, out onto the battlements of the great tower. There he faced toward the west where lay a new moon, louting toward the setting sun; and he laid the two robes, one on either arm, spreading them abroad, till they looked like two wings—a gold and a pearl. And a beam of the sun came and kissed the gold wing, and a pale quivering thread of moonlight touched the pearl wing; and Gammelyn sang:

"Light of the moon,
Light of the sun,
Pearl of the sky,
Gold from on high,
Hearken to me!

"Light of the moon,
Pearl of the sea,
Gold of the land
Here in my hand,
I render to thee.

"Butterflies come!
Carry us home,
Gold of the gnome,
Pearl of the sea."

And as he sang, out of the east came a soft muttering of wings and a deep moving mass like a bright storm-cloud. And out of the sun ran a long gold finger, and out of the moon a pale shivering finger of pearl, and touching the gold and the pearl, these became verily wings and not of dresses. Then before the Princess could scream more than once or the King say anything about cutting off heads, the bright cloud in the east became a myriad myriad of butterflies. And drawn by the falling flashing sun and by the faint falling moon and fanned by the million wings of his fellow creatures, Gammelyn sprang out from the palace wall on the crest of the butterfly wind, and flew away brighter and farther each moment; and followed by his myriad train of butterflies, he passed out of sight, and in that country was never heard of again.

———◆·●————

FOUR

The Traveller's Shoes

A long while ago there lived a young cobbler named Lubin, who, when his father died, was left with only the shop and the shoe-leather out of which to make his fortune. From morning to night he toiled, making and mending the shoes of the poor village folk; but his earnings were small, and he seemed never able to get more than three days ahead of poverty.

One day as he sat working at his window-bench, the door opened and in came a traveller. He had on a pair of long red shoes with pointed ends; but of one the seams had split, so that all his toes were coming out of it.

The stranger, putting up one foot after the other, took off both shoes, and giving that one which wanted cobbling to Lubin, he said: "Tonight I shall be sleep-

ing here at the inn; have this ready in good time tomorrow, for I am in haste to go on!" And having said this he put the other shoe into his pocket and went out of the door barefoot.

"What a funny fellow," thought Lubin, "not to make the most of one shoe when he has it!" But without stopping to puzzle himself he took up the to-be-mended shoe and set to work. When it was finished he threw it down on the floor behind him and went on working at his other jobs. He meant to work late, for he had not enough money yet to get himself his Sunday's dinner; so when darkness shut in, he lighted a rushlight and cobbled away, thinking to himself all the while of the roast meat that was to be his reward.

It came close on midnight, and he was just putting on the last heel of the last pair of shoes when he was aware of a noise on the floor behind him. He looked round, and there was the red shoe with the pointed toe, cutting capers and prancing about by itself in the middle of the room.

"Peace on earth!" exclaimed Lubin. "I never saw a shoe do a thing so tipsy before!" He went up and passed his hand over it and under it, but there was nothing to account for its caperings; on it went, up and down, toeing and heeling, skipping and sliding, as if for a very wager. Lubin could even tell himself the name of the reel and the tune that it was dancing to, for all that the other foot was missing. Presently the shoe tripped and toppled, falling heel up upon the floor; nor, although

Lubin watched it for a full hour, did it ever start upon a fresh jig.

Soon after daybreak, when Lubin had but just opened his shutters and sat himself down to work, in came the traveller, limping upon bare feet, with the shoe's fellow pointing its red toe out of his pocket. "Oh, so," he said, seeing the other shoe ready mended and waiting for him, "how much am I owing you for the job?"

"Just a gold piece," said Lubin, carelessly, carrying on at his work.

"A gold piece for the mere mending of a shoe!" cried the stranger. "You must be either a rogue or a funny fellow."

"Neither!" said Lubin, "and for mending a shoe my charge is only a penny; but for mending *that* shoe, and for all the worry and temptation to make it my own and run off with it—a gold piece!"

"To be sure, you are an honest fellow," said the traveller, "and honesty is a rare gift; though, had you made off with it, I should have soon caught you. Still, you were not so wise as to know that, so here's your gold piece for you." He pulled out a big bag of gold as he spoke, pouring its contents out on the window bench.

"That is a lot of money for a lonely man to carry about," said Lubin. "Are you not afraid?"

"Why, no," answered the man. "I have a way, so that I can always follow it up even if I lose it." He took two of the gold pieces and dropped one into the sole

of each shoe as he was putting them on. "There!" said he, "now, if any man steal my money, I need only wait till it is midnight; and then I have but to say to my shoes, 'Seek!' and up they jump, with me in them, and carry me to where my stolen property is, were it to the world's end. It is as if they had the nose and sagacity of a pair of bloodhounds. Ah, son of a cobbler, had you run off with the one, I should have very soon caught you with the other; for if one walks, the other is bound to follow. But, as you were honest, we part friends; and I trust God may bring you to fortune." Then the traveller did up his bag of gold, nodded to the cobbler from the doorway, and was gone.

Lubin laid down his work and went off to the inn. "Did anything happen here last night?" he asked.

"Nothing of much note," answered the innkeeper. "Three travelling fiddlers were here, and afterwards a man came in barefoot, but with a red shoe sticking out of his pocket. I thought of turning the fellow away, till he let me see the color of his gold. Presently the fiddlers started to play and the other man to drink. At first when they called on him to dance he excused himself for his feet's sake; but presently, what with the music and the liquor, he got so lively in his head that he pulled on his shoe and danced like three ordinary men put together."

"What time was that?" asked Lubin.

"Getting on for midnight," answered the innkeeper.

"Ah!" said Lubin, and went home thinking much on the way.

Toward evening he found that he had run out of

leather and must go into the town, ten miles off, to buy more. "Now my gold piece comes in handy" thought he; so he locked up the house, put the key in his pocket, and set out.

Though it was the season of long days, it was growing dark when he came to a part of the road that led through the wood; but being so poor a man he had no fear, nor thought at all about the robbers who were said to be in those parts. But as he went, he saw all at once by the side of the road two red spikes sticking up out of a ditch, their bright color making them plain to the eye. He came quite near and saw that they were two red shoes with pointed toes; and then he saw more clearly that along with them lay the traveller, his wallet empty and with a dagger stuck through his heart.

The cobbler's son was as sorry as he could be. "Alas, poor soul," thought he, "what good are the shoes to you now? Now that thieves have killed you and taken away your gold, surely I do no harm if I give an honest man your shoes!" He stooped down and was about taking them off when he saw the eyes of the dead man open. The eyes looked at him as if they would remind him of something; and at once, when he loosed hold of the shoes, they seemed satisfied. Then he remembered and thought to himself, "The world has many marvels in it; I will wait till midnight and see."

For over three hours he kept watch by the dead man's side. "Only last night," he said to himself, "this poor fellow was dancing as merry a measure as ever I saw, for the half of it surely I saw; and now!" Then he

judged that midnight must be come, so he bent over the shoes and whispered to them but one word.

The dead man stood up in his shoes and began running. Lubin followed close, keeping an eye on him, for the shoes made no sound on the earth. They ran on for two hours, till they had come to the thickest part of the forest; then some way before them Lubin began to see a light shining. It came from a small square house in a courtyard, and round the courtyard lay a deep moat; only one narrow plank led over and up to the entrance.

The red shoes, carrying the dead man, walked over, and Lubin followed them. When they were at the other side, they turned, facing toward the plank that they had crossed, and Lubin seemed to read in the dead man's eye what he was to do.

Then he turned and lifted the plank away from over the moat, so that there was no longer any entrance or exit to the place. Through the window of the house he could see the three fiddlers quarrelling over the dead man's gold.

The red shoes went on, carrying their dead owner, till they got to the threshold, and there stopped. Then Lubin came and clicked up the latch and pushed open the door, and in walked the dead man with the dagger sticking out of his heart.

The three fiddlers, when they saw that sight, dropped their gold and leapt out of the window; and as they fled, shrieking, thinking to cross the moat by the plank-bridge that was no longer there, one after the other

they fell into the water and, clutching each other by the throat, were drowned.

But the red shoes stayed where they were and, tilting up his feet, let the traveller go gently upon the ground; and when Lubin held down the lantern to his face, on it lay a good smile to tell him that the dead man thanked him for all he had done.

So in the morning Lubin went and fetched a priest to pray for the repose of the traveller's soul and to give him good burial; and to him he gave all the dead man's money, but for himself he took the red shoes with the pointed toes and set out to make his fortune in the world.

Walking along he found that however far he went he never grew tired. When he had gone on for more than a hundred miles, he came to the capital where the King lived with his Court.

All the flags of the city were at half-mast, and all the people were in half-mourning. Lubin asked at the first inn where he stopped what it all meant.

"You must indeed be a stranger," said his host, "not to know, for 'tis now nearly a year since this trouble began; and this very night more cause for mourning becomes due."

"Tell me of it, then," said Lubin, "for I know nothing at all."

"At least," returned the innkeeper, "you will know how, a little more than a year ago, the Queen, who was the most beautiful woman in the world, died, leaving the King with twelve daughters, who, after her,

were reckoned the fairest women on earth, though the
King says that all their beauty rolled into one would
not equal that of his dead wife; and, indeed, poor man,
there is no doubt that he loved her devotedly during
her life and mourns for her continually now she is
dead."

"Only a small part of all this have I known," said
Lubin.

"Well, but at least," said the innkeeper, "you will
have heard how the Princesses were famed for their hair;
so beautiful it was, so golden, and so long! And now,
at every full moon, one of them goes bald in a night; and
bald her head stays as a stone, for never an inch of
hair grows on it again; and with her hair all her beauty
goes pale, so that she is but the shadow of her former
self—a thin-blooded thing, as if a vampire had come
and sucked out half her life. Yes; ten months this has
happened, and ten of the Princesses have lost their looks
and their hair as well; and now only the Princess Royal
and the youngest of all remain untouched; and doubtless
one of them is to lose her crop tonight."

"But how does it happen?" cried Lubin. "Is no one
put to keep watch, to guard them from the thing being
done?"

"Ah! you talk, you talk!" said the innkeeper. "How?
The King has offered half his kingdom to anyone who
can tell him how the mischief is done; and the other
half to the man who will put an end to it. To put it
shortly, if you believe yourself a clever enough man,
you may have the King for your father-in-law, with the

pick of his daughters for your bride, and be his heir and lord of all when he dies!"

"For such a reward," said Lubin, "has no man made the attempt?"

"Aye, one a month; every time there has been some man fool enough to think himself so clever; and he has been turned out of the palace next day with his ears cropped."

"I will risk having my ears cropped," said Lubin; for his heart was sorry for the young Princesses and the vanishing of their beauty. So he went up and knocked at the gates of the palace.

They went and told the King that a new man had come willing and wanting to have his ears cropped on the morrow. "Well, well," said the King, "let the poor fool in!" for indeed he had given up all hope. From the King, Lubin heard the whole story over again. The old man sighed so it took him whole hours to tell it.

"I would be glad to be your son," said Lubin, when the King had ended, "but I would like better to make you rid of your sorrow."

"That is kind of you," said the King. "Perhaps I will only crop one of your ears tomorrow."

"When may one see the Princesses?" asked Lubin.

"They will be down to supper presently," answered the King, "then you shall see them, what there is left of them."

Though it was reckoned that the next day Lubin would have to be drummed out of the palace with his ears cropped short, on this day he was to be treated

like an honored guest. When they went in to supper, the King made him sit upon his right hand.

The twelve Princesses came in, their heads bowed down with weeping; all were fair, but ten of them were thin and pale and wore white wimples over their heads like nuns; only the Princess Royal, who was the eldest, and Princess Lyneth, who was the youngest, had gold hair down to their feet and were both so shiningly beautiful that the poor cobbler was altogether dazzled by the sight of them.

The King looked out of the window and said: "Heigho! There is the full moon beginning to rise." Then they all said grace and sat down.

But when the viands were handed round, all the Princesses sat weeping into their plates and seemed unable to eat anything. For the pale and thin ones said: "Tonight another of our sisters will lose her golden hair and her good looks and be like us!" Therefore they wept.

And Lyneth said: "Tonight, either my dear sister or myself will fall under the spell!" Therefore she wept more than the other ten. But the Princess Royal sat trembling and crying:

"Tonight I know that the curse is to fall upon me, and me only!" Therefore she wept more than all.

Lubin sat, and watched, and listened, with his head bent down over his golden plate. "Which of these two shall I try most to save?" he thought. "How shall I test them, so as to know? If I could only tell which of

them was to lose her hair tonight, then I might do something."

He saw that the youngest sister cried so much that she could eat nothing; but the Princess Royal, between her bursts of grief, picked up a morsel now and again from her plate and ate it as though courage or despair reminded her that she must yet strive to live.

When the meat courses were over, the King said to the Princess: "I wish you would try to eat a little pudding! Here is a very promising youth, who is determined by all that is in him that harm shall happen to none of you tonight."

"Tomorrow he will be sent away with his ears cut short!" said Princess Lyneth; and her tears, as she spoke, ran down over the edge of her plate onto the cloth.

When supper was over, the Princess Royal came up to Lubin and said: "Do not be angry with my sister for what she said! It has only been too true of many who came before; tonight, unless you do better than them all, I shall lose my hair. It has been a wonder to me how I have been spared so long, seeing that I am the eldest and, as some will have it, the fairest. Will you keep a good guard over me tonight, as though you knew for certain that I am to be the one this time to suffer?"

"I will guard you as my own life," said Lubin, "if you will but do as I ask you."

"Pledge yourself to me, then, in this cup!" said she, and lifted to his lips a bowl of red wine. Over the edge

of it her eyes shone beautifully; he drank gazing into their clear depth.

"Where am I to be for the night," he asked of the King, "so that I may watch over the two Princesses?"

The King took him to a chamber with two further doors that opened out of it. "Here," said the King, "you are to sleep, and in the inner rooms sleep the Princess Royal and the Princess Lyneth. There is no entrance or exit to them but through this; therefore, when you are here with your door bolted, one would suppose that you had them safe. Alas! ten other men have tried like you to ward off the harm and have failed; and so today I have ten daughters with no looks left to them and no hair upon their heads."

As they were speaking, the two Princesses, with their sisters, came up to bed. And the pale ones, wearing their white wimples, came and kissed the golden hair of the other two, crying over it, and saying, "To one of you we are saying good-bye; tomorrow one of you will be like us!" Then they went away to their sleeping-place, and the Princess Royal and Lyneth kissed each other and parted weeping, each into her own chamber.

"Watch well over us!" said Lyneth to Lubin, as she passed through. "Watch over me!" said the Princess Royal. And then the two doors were closed.

Lubin said to the King, "Could I now see the two Princesses, without being seen by them, it would help me to know what to do."

"Come down to my cabinet," said the King. "I have an invisible cap there, that I can lend you if you think

you can do any good with it." So they went; and the King reached down the cap from the wall and gave it to Lubin.

"Now, good night, your Majesty," said Lubin; "I will do for you all I can."

The King answered, "Either you shall be my son-in-law tomorrow, or you shall have no ears. My wishes are with you that the former state may be yours."

Lubin went into his chamber and closed and bolted the door; then he put the bed up against it. "Now, at least," he thought, "there are three of us, and no more!" He put on his invisible cap, and going softly to the Princess Royal's door, opened it and peeped in.

She stood up before her glass, combing out her long gold hair and smiling proudly because of its beauty. She gathered it up by all its ends and kissed it; then, letting it fall, she went on combing as before.

Lubin went out, closing the door again; then he took off his cap and knocked, and presently he heard the Princess Royal saying, "Come in!" She was lying down upon the bed, squeezing her eyes with her hands.

"Princess," he said, "I will watch over you like my own life, if you will do what I bid you. I am but a poor man, and the best that I can do is but poor; but I think, if you will, I can save your head from becoming as bare as a billiard ball."

The Princess asked him how.

"You know," said he, "that tonight something is to happen to one of you" ("To me!" said the Princess), "and all your hair will be stolen in such a way that noth-

ing will ever make it grow again. See, here I have a pair of common scissors; let me but cut your hair close off all over your head, and then who can steal it? For a few months you will be a fright, but it can grow again."

"I think you are a silly fellow!" said the Princess. "Better for you to get to bed and have your ears cropped quietly in the morning! After all, it may be my sister's turn to lose her hair, not mine. I shall not make myself a fright for a year of my life in order to save you."

"If you think so poorly of my offer," said Lubin, "I had better go to bed and sleep and not trouble the Princess Lyneth at all with it."

"No, indeed!" said the Princess Royal. "Go to bed and sleep, poor fool!" And, in truth, Lubin was feeling so sleepy that he could hardly keep open his eyes.

Then he left her and, pulling the invisible cap once more over his head, crept softly into Princess Lyneth's chamber.

She was standing before her glass with all her beautiful hair flowing down from shoulders to feet; and tears were falling fast out of her eyes as she kept drawing her hair together in her hands, kissing and moaning over it.

Then Lubin went out again and, taking off his cap, knocked softly at the door.

"Come in!" said the Princess; and when he went in she was still standing before the glass weeping and moaning for her beautiful hair that might never see another day. On the bed was lying a white wimple, ready for her to put on when her head was become bald.

"Princess," said Lubin, very humbly, "will you help me to save your beautiful hair, by doing what I ask?"

"What is it that you ask?" said she.

"Only this," he answered; "I am a poor man and cannot do much for you, but only my best. Tonight you or your sister must lose your hair; and we know that afterwards, if that happen, it can never grow again. Now, come, here I have a common pair of scissors; if I could cut your hair quite short, in a few months it will grow again, and there will be nothing tonight that the Fates can steal. Will you let me do this for you in true service?"

The Princess looked at him and looked at her glass. "Oh, my hair, my hair!" she moaned. Then she said, "What matters it? You mean to be good to me, and a month is the most that my fortune can last. If I do not lose it tonight, I lose it at the next full moon!" Then she shut her eyes and bade him take off all he wished. When he had finished, she picked up the wimple and covered her head with it; but Lubin took up the long coil of gold hair and wound it round his heart.

He knelt down at her feet. "Princess," he said, "be sure now that I can save you! Only I have one other request to make."

"What is that?" asked the Princess.

He took off one of his red shoes with the pointed toes. "Will you, for a strange thing, put on this shoe and wear it all tonight in your sleep? And in the morning I will ask you for it again."

The Princess promised faithfully that she would

do so. Even before he had left the room she had put foot in it, promising that only he should take it off again.

Lubin's eyes were shut down with sleep as he groped his way to bed; he lay down with the other red shoe upon his foot. "Watch for your fellow!" he said to it; and then his senses left him and he was fast asleep.

In the middle of the night, while he was deep in slumber, the red shoe caught him by the foot and yanked him out of bed; he woke up to find himself standing in the middle of the room, and there before him stood the two doors of the inner chambers open; through that of the Princess Royal came a light. He heard the Princess Lyneth getting very softly out of her bed, and presently she stood in the doorway, with her hands out and her eyes fast shut; and the red shoe was on one foot and the white wimple on her head. Little tears were running down from under her closed lids; and she sighed continually in her sleep. "Have pity on me!" she said.

She crossed slowly from one door to the other; and Lubin, putting on his invisible cap, crept softly after her. The Princess Royal's chamber was empty, but her glass was opened away from the wall like a door, and beyond lay a passage and steps. At the top of the steps was another door, and through it light came and the sound of a soft voice singing.

Princess Lyneth, knowing nothing in her sleep, passed along the passage and up the steps till she came to the further doorway. Looking over her shoulder

Lubin saw the Princess Royal sitting before a loom. In it lay a great cloth of gold, like a bride's mantle, into which she was weaving the last threads of her skein. Close to her side lay a pair of great shears that shone like blue fire; and while she sang they opened and snapped, keeping time to the music she made.

Without ever turning her head the Princess Royal sat passing her fingers along the woof and crying:

"Sister, sister, bring me your hair,
    Of our Mother's beauty give me your share.
    You must grow pale, while I must grow fair!"

And while she was so singing, Lyneth drew nearer and nearer, with her eyes fast shut, and the white wimple over her head. "Have pity on me!" she said, speaking in her sleep.

As soon as the Princess Royal heard that, she laughed for joy, and catching up the great flaming shears, turned herself round to where Lyneth was standing. Then she opened the shears and took hold of the wimple and pulled it down.

All in a moment she was choking with rage, for horrible was the sight that met her eye. "Ah! cobbler's son," cried she, "you shall die for this! Tomorrow not only shall you have your two ears cropped, but you shall die: do not be afraid!"

Lubin looked at her and smiled, knowing how little she thought that he heard her words. "Ah! Princess Royal," he said to himself, "there is another who should now be afraid, but is not."

Then for very spite the Princess began slapping her sister's face. "Ah! wicked little sister," she cried, "you have cheated me this time! But go back and wait till your hair has grown, and then my gown of gold shall be finished, although this once you have been too sly!" She threw down the shears and drove her sister back by stair and passage and through the looking-glass door at the other end.

Lubin following, stayed first to watch how by a secret spring the Princess Royal closed the mirror back into the wall; then he slipped on before, and taking his cap off, lay down on his bed pretending to be fast asleep. He heard Princess Lyneth return to her couch, and then came the Princess Royal and ground her teeth at him in the darkness.

Presently she, too, returned to her bed and lay down; and an hour after Lubin got up very softly and went into her chamber. There she lay asleep, with her beautiful hair all spread out upon the pillow; but Lubin had Princess Lyneth's hair wound round his heart. He touched the secret spring, so that the mirror opened to him, and he passed through toward the little chamber where stood the loom.

There hung the cloth of gold, all but finished; beside it the shears opened and snapped, giving out a blue light. He took up the shears in his hand, and pulled down the gold web from the loom, and back he went, closing the mirror behind him.

Then he came to the Princess Royal as she lay asleep; and first he laid the cloth of gold over her and

saw how at once she became ten times more fair than she was by rights, as fair almost as her dead mother, lacking one part only. But her beauty did not win him to have pity on her.

"There can be thieves, it seems, in high places!" he said; and with that he opened the shears over her head and let them snap: then all her long hair came out by the roots and she lay white and withered before his eyes and as bald as a stone.

He gathered up all her hair with one hand, and the cloth of gold with the other, and went quietly away. Then, hiding the shears in a safe place, first he burnt the Princess Royal's hair, till it became only a little heap of frizzled cinders; and after that he went to the chamber of the ten Princesses, whose hair and whose sweet youth had been stolen from them. There they lay all in a row in ten beds, with pale, gentle faces, asleep under their white wimples.

He went to the first and, laying the cloth of hair over her, cried:

"Sister, sister, I bring you your hair,
 Of your Mother's beauty I give you your share.
 One must grow pale, but you must grow fair!"

And as he said the words one part of the cloth un-wove itself from the rest and ran in ripples up the coverlet and on to the pillow where the Princess's head lay. There it coiled itself under the wimple, a great mass of shining gold, and the face of the Princess flushed warm and lovely in her sleep.

Lubin passed on to the next bed, and there uttered the same words; and again one part of the web came loose and wound itself about the sleeper's face that grew warm and lovely at its touch. So he went from bed to bed, and when he came to the end there was no more of the web left.

He went back into his own chamber, laughing in his heart for joy, and there he dropped himself between the sheets and fell into a sound slumber.

He was awakened in the morning by the King knocking and trying to get into the room. Lubin pulled back the bed, and in came the King with a mournful countenance.

"Which of them is it?" said he.

"Go and ask them!" said Lubin.

The King went over and knocked at the Princess Royal's door: the knocking opened her eyes. Lubin heard her suddenly utter a yell. "Ah! now she has looked at herself in the glass," thought he.

"What is the matter?" called the King. "Come out and let me look at you!" But the Princess Royal would not come out. She ran quick to her mirror and touched the secret spring. "At least," she thought, "though fiends have robbed me of all my beauty, I can get it back by wearing the cloth woven from my sisters' hair!" She skipped along the passage and up the steps to the little chamber where the loom was.

The King, getting no answer, went across and knocked at Lyneth's door; she came out, all fresh in her beauty, but wearing upon her head the wimple.

"Ah!" said the King dolorously; and he snipped his fingers at Lubin.

Lubin laughed out. "But look at her face!" he said. "Surely she is beautiful enough?"

The Princess lifted up her wimple and showed the King her hair all shorn beneath. "That was my doing," said Lubin; " 'twas the way of saving it."

"What a Dutchman's remedy!" cried the King; and just then the Princess Royal's door flew open.

She came out tearing herself to pieces with rage; her face was pale and thin, and her head was as bare as a billiard ball. "Have that clown of a cobbler killed!" she cried in a passion. "That fool, that numbskull, that cheat! Have him beheaded, I say!"

"No, no, I am only to have one of my ears cropped off!" said Lubin, looking hard at her all the time.

"I am not at all sure," said the King. "You have done foolishly and badly, for not only have you let the disease go on, but your very remedy is as bad. Two heads of hair gone in one night! You had better have kept away. If the Princesses wish it, certainly I will have you put to death."

"Will you not see the other Princesses too?" asked Lubin. "Let them decide between them whether I am to live or die!"

The King was just going to call for them, when suddenly the ten Princesses opened the door of their chamber and stood before him shining like stars, with all their golden hair running down to their feet.

"Now put me to death!" said Lubin; and all the time

he kept his eye upon the Princess Royal, who turned flame-colored with rage.

"No, indeed!" cried the King. "Now you must be more than pardoned! You see, my dears," he said to Lyneth and the Princess Royal, "though you have suffered, your sisters have recovered all that they lost. They are ten to two; and I can't go back on arithmetic; I am bound to do even more than pardon him for this."

"Indeed and indeed yes!" replied the Princess Lyneth. "He has done ten times more than we thought of asking him!" And she went from one to another of her recovered sisters, kissing their beautiful long hair for pure gladness of heart. But when she came to the Princess Royal, she kissed her many times and stooped down her face upon her shoulder and cried over her.

"Tell me now," said the King to Lubin, "for you are a very wonderful fellow, how did it all happen?"

Lubin looked at the Princess Royal; after all he could not betray a lady's secret. "I cannot tell you," he said; "if I did, there would be a death in the family."

"Well," said the King, "however you may have done it, I own that you have earned your reward. You have only to choose now which of my daughters is to make you my son-in-law. From this day you shall be known as my heir." He ranged all the Princesses in line, according to their ages. "Now choose," said the King, "and choose well!"

Lubin went up to the Princess Royal. "I won't have you!" he said, looking very hard at her; and the Princess Royal dropped her eyes. Then he went on to the next.

"Sweet lady," he said, "I dare not ask one with such beautiful hair as yours to marry me, who am a poor cobbler's son." But all the while he had the Princess Lyneth's hair bound round his heart.

He went on from one to another, and of each he kissed the hand, saying that she was too fair to marry him.

He came to Lyneth and knelt down at her feet. "Lyneth," he said, "will you give the poor cobbler back his shoe?"

Lyneth, looking in his eyes, saw all that he meant. "And myself in it," she said, "for you love me dearly!" She put her arms round his neck and whispered, "You marry me because I am a fright and have no hair!"

But Lubin said, "I have your hair all wound round my heart, making it warm!"

So they were married and lived together more happily than cobbler and princess ever lived in the world before. And the cobbler dropped mending shoes: only his wife's shoes he always mended. Very soon Lyneth's hair grew again, more shining and beautiful than before; but the Princess Royal remained pale and thin and was bald to the day of her death.

—◆·◆—

FIVE

The Wooing
of the Maze

Once upon a time there lived a beautiful Princess named Rosemary who had all she wanted in the world but freedom. She had riches and power and glory without end; but above and beyond all these things, her beauty was like the sound of a trumpet.

If she lifted the veil from her face or looked out from her window at morning as she combed her bright hair, the whole plain at her feet became like an army of banners, and the hillsides dark with the galloping of her suitors.

Rejected potentates went clamoring to the four winds of heaven of her charm and of her cruelty; and the saying went that she had paved the floor of her palace with the hearts which she had broken.

But she was weary, was weary of saying "No" to

wooers she did not love; and often when alone she would cry that her riches and her power and her glory might vanish away from her, and her beauty too, save so much of it as would win her the heart of the one man she loved and leave her to be tended by his hands, as was her sweet namesake rosemary.

One day at noon, when it was the middle of summer, she was lying on a couch in the palace watching how the flies' wings threw a network on the air as they made love to each other and played. It seemed to her so like the net that the swarm of her suitors threw round her day by day that she caught one of the flies, and to make it more like herself, sprinkled it with gold dust so that it shone; then she let it go. But to her surprise all the other flies avoided it, and the gilded one went about solitary and alone.

"Oh! why then," she cried, "am I not left free like yonder fly sprinkled with gold?"

Just then under the window a young gardener at his work among the flowers began singing; and this is what he sang:

> "What will I do for my rose of the roses?
>   Build her a window that looks at the sky;
> Fashion her bower with a door that so closes,
>   No man shall open or enter but I."

The Princess waited till the words of the song were ended; then a smile broke over her face; she took up her guitar, and with musically skilled fingers played over the air as it had been sung. One by one the clear notes

sprang through the open window and fell upon the ears of the listener on the green lawn below. Also her voice took up the air and sang:

"Thus, in her heart, saith thy rose of the roses,
  Build me a window with heaven for its brow;
Fashion my bower with a door that so closes,
  No man shall open or enter but thou."

That same day the Princess, sitting upon her throne and having crown and scepter in her hands, caused the gardener to be called into her presence. The courtiers thought it was very strange that the Princess should have a thing of such importance to make known to a gardener that it was necessary for her to receive him with crown and throne and scepter, as if it were an affair of state.

To the gardener, when he stood before her, she said, "Gardener, it is my wish that there should be fashioned for me a very great maze, so intricate and deceitful that no man who has not the secret of it shall be able to penetrate therein. Inmost is to be a little tower and fountains and borders of sweet-smelling flowers and herbs. But the man who fashions this maze and has its secret must remain in it forever lest he should betray his knowledge to others. So it is my will that you should devise such a maze for my delight and be yourself the prisoner of your own craft when it is accomplished."

The gardener lifted his head where he knelt and saw the Princess sitting with eyes fast shut and hard-

bitten lips and hands down loose on either side of her, from which had fallen the crown and scepter they had held. Then he answered her, "Princess, by all the might of my craft I will be, and it shall be so as you wish."

Now the Princess gave it out to the world that, being so wooed, she was minded to put all men who required her hand to a great test, that so he who deserved her most might win her. Therefore at such and such a time she made it to be known that she would withdraw herself from all men's eyes to the center of a great maze strongly knit round by magic, and that whoever desired her beauty and could penetrate through all the deceits and dangers of that maze should possess herself and her lands and her power and live in glory of his achievement.

Day by day, out of her palace window, she watched the great maze as it grew. Wondrously it wound like a huge serpent, gathering into its fold many miles of country—wood and hill and valley, and great pits and caverns. And far within rose a small round tower about which stood fountains like silver willows blown by the wind; but the door no man could see, for mighty hedges and walls circled all ways about, cutting off what was below the eye, so that the inner garden lay hidden like a skylark's nest in the corn.

One day when the Princess asked, "How strong is this maze to be?" the gardener answered, "As strong as love." And when she asked, "How hard will its way be to find?" he answered, "As hard as is the foolishness

of the kings and princes who shall seek thee therein."
Then she laughed and was comforted in her heart when
the day approached on which all the world was to be
parted from her.

On that day a hundred suitors had gathered to the
Court, eager to prove their prowess and win the most
beautiful woman in all the world for a bride. At night
the palace was ablaze from floor to roof, for there a
great feast was held, at which sat Princess Rosemary,
magnificent in her beauty and the splendor of her robes
and crown. And all the kings and princes and lords
bent round her with love and worship.

When the clocks struck midnight she rose, and all
her jewels shone in the fashion of a star, so thickly
clustered the eye might not discern one from other;
but from heel to crown they clothed her as in a sheet
of fire. She passed down the midst of the hall, bowing
both ways to the assembly in gracious farewell, and
her train as it went from floor to floor was as a great
retinue following her when she herself had passed forth.

She went from terrace to terrace of garden under
great trees where torches and trombones hung, blown
by the wind, till she came to the entrance of the maze.
Then she drew out of her breast a small chart, and gazing thereon went as though fate-led out of sight and
sound. And all the crowd standing without watched
the mysterious jeweled train of her robe passing in
after she was gone, as though itself knew the way it
had to go and the windings that led into the very heart
of the maze. A whispered tale went from mouth to

mouth that he who had devised and fashioned the maze had disappeared—was dead, lest the secret should be betrayed. Some said, "Poison"; some said nothing, but shook their heads darkly and seemed wise.

At the first dawn of day the hundred kings, princes, and knights went forth to the wooing of the maze, for there were many paths, and each one went his own way.

For many days the doors remained sealed and silent as a tomb, and the crowds that gathered daily to watch began dwindling away, and went back to resume their neglected trades. At last the countries whose kings did not return sent ambassadors with messages that became more and more urgent in demanding their presence. They spoke of the balance of thrones, and the encroachments of neighboring powers, and the deaths of relatives. These ambassadors went down to the various entrances at which their masters had been seen to go in and thence shot arrows at a venture with the urgent messages attached to them. But yet none came to answer.

Then the ambassadors were summoned away, for new kings had seized on the vacant thrones, and the return of their predecessors became no longer expedient. People almost forgot at last to trouble their heads, save when fresh suitors came desirous of joining in the great wooing of the maze, the more by reason of its apparent dangers. Then indeed for a time gossips would wait and talk, but afterward they went away.

Many years went by, and at last there came forth a knight with grizzled hair and bowed head. He walked

in loops and circles, and his eyes slid from right to left over the ground at his feet. He seemed crazed and stuttered when he spoke. They asked him how he had fared. He showed them many badges of other knights fastened about his shield and helmet. "I overthrew these," he said, "till I met one who said, 'I am Old Age: turn back!' "

They watched after him with his middle-aged stoop, till he had stumbled his way into his own country. Some remembered him as a gallant young knight fifteen years ago.

Yet the story went that the wondrous beauty of the Princess did not fade; and the people became proud of a legend that spread so great a distinction for their land and would point to the maze and the far-off fountains and say, "There waits our beautiful Princess till one come worthy to woo her."

Twenty years had gone by when one day a goodly young Prince, with a smiling countenance, and two long lances slung over his back, made his appearance at the palace and demanded admittance to the maze. Half the population streamed out to meet him, for it was many years since the last wooer had come and vanished never to return. The country remembered its importance, and gave him a great welcome. "Look what long lances he has!" shouted the crowd. And then the doors of the maze closed on him, and they went back to their work.

When the Prince had made some way into the maze, he fastened his horse to a tree, took down his

lances and—chopped off their points. Lo, and behold! he had turned them into stilts, great high stilts, so that by mounting them he could see far away over the windings of the maze into the very heart of it.

Far off he could see the silver glint of fountains like gray willows blown slantwise in the wind. That way with a pleasant tune in his heart he straddled merrily along. If he found himself in a blind alley, or being carried back by the windings of the road, he stood on one stilt and went "leg over" with the other; thus his goings prospered.

Here and there, he came upon dead men lying in their armor; some of them were quite old, others had long lances by their sides; they must have been hard of understanding and foolish. He passed them all by.

For the whole long day he traveled, till toward evening he came upon a little wood and saw through the tree boles the gray stones of the little tower and felt on his face the spray of the fountains carried by the wind. Also he heard the sound of pleasant voices and the stroke of a spade in the earth.

Free of the wood, the path led straight on, till at the end of it, over a high hedge, lay a dainty bright garden. A man and a woman were bending together over a border of flowers. Their faces were close together, full of smiles as their hands gathered sprays of rosemary; their hair was wet with the drift of the fountains.

Both were in the early middle-age of life, the woman tall and broad-bosomed, her hair like a plaited crown of gold.

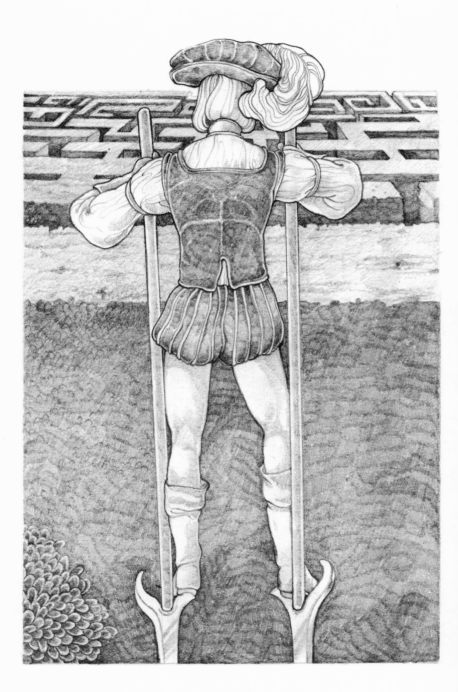

The man, as her face brushed his, laughed and began singing:

"What shall I do for my rose of the roses?
Build her a window that looks at the sky,
Fashion a door to her bower that so closes,
No man shall open or enter but I."

The Prince came and looked over the hedge; at the end of the song the gardener and his wife had raised themselves; the woman had her face resting on the man's shoulder and her arms about his waist. As she stood, her eyes came straight upon the intruder, who hung a laughing head and shoulders over the garden hedge. Her mouth and eyes went wide open, but breath was wanting for speech. She pinched her husband to make him look round.

The Prince, smiling, addressed them with the utmost courtesy, "Good Sir and Madam, can you tell me whether the Princess is at home?" As he spoke he lifted a stilt and planted it down on the flower bed inside. One more stride and he was in. There was a sudden clapping of hands. "He's a humorist!" cried the gardener's wife.

"Please," said he, as he climbed down from his height and stood once more on his own feet, "please, I am come for the Princess; and I hope she is not tired of waiting and is as beautiful and as young as report has led me to believe."

The gardener's wife laughed and ran into the tower. Presently from roof to floor it was filled with a great rustling sound, and all the windows shone with the

color of fire. Then out of the door came a lovely girl blazing with jewels and drawing behind her a wonderful great train. "Here is your Princess," said her mother. How beautiful she was, how radiant, how young! She came softly toward the Prince, laughing and holding out her hand. He took it, and as he did so the whole of the maze disappeared, and only the little tower with its fountains remained. So the young couple went back to the palace and were married, but the other couple stayed at home; and there they lived happily ever after.

——◆·◆——

SIX

Moozipoo

The Story of the White Hare of the Yabloni Mountains

It was midwinter; the snow had come down from the north like a white wall on the march and, falling upon villages and outlying settlements, had buried them so deep that even from the roof there was no outlook for the eye; and scarcely a man in the whole community dare stir abroad. The people shut up in their houses were beginning to starve, and still the snow fell.

Old Sveljik, the head man of the largest of the Yabloni villages, was the father of nine strong sons; but even they, great hunters though they were, had laid by their bows and their hunting spears and sat all day at home.

At last one day, old Sveljik, seeing the sky still dark with falling snow, said: "Surely we have offended the Snowers, the white hill tribe, and they are now sending

war on us. If that be so, there is but one thing that can end it."

"What will end it?" inquired his nine sons. And their father answered, "I am chief here, and we are ten men. If between you, you can kill ten white hares and bring their skins home as trophies, then you will have taken good payment, and they will give us peace instead of war; but not one of you is hunter enough, and I am grown old."

His sons said: "Tomorrow when it gets light, we will go out and seek; and if there are but ten white hares in all the world, we will bring their skins back with us."

But without saying anything to the rest, Helnar, the youngest of them, as soon as his brethren were asleep, rose up softly, and putting on his snowshoes, went out alone into the night.

No snow was falling then, and the moon shone bright as day; and Helnar set his face to the north, toward the hollow center of the hills out of which the snow came down to the plains.

"Surely it is yonder," said he, "if at all that I shall find them; for it was there last moon that I found, caught in a trap, the white doe hare that spoke to me, and which indeed for pity I let go. But tonight, I must not wait to know if what I would kill has a voice to beg life of me."

After a while, gliding swiftly with firm feet, he had come to the hollows of the hills, where the moon shadows lay like black pits in the snow, but he could see no life moving anywhere.

Every trace of living things seemed to have been

buried out of sight, not a footprint of bird or beast was on the snow's surface through all the miles he had come.

Presently the moon sunk dim into a fresh bank of clouds; a snapping wind came worrying through the rocks and the ravines, shouldering the white drifts; and again the snow came, filling the air, thick and fast, spinning and curling, this way and that, so that Helnar could no longer see or tell in which direction he was going.

For hours and hours he went on, like a man wool-gathering, and the fresh snow grew soft and yielding so that his feet sank in it and were hard to get free again.

At last, he became so weary that he could scarcely bend a knee or lift a leg; and still the snow swung round him like a huge winding-sheet, making a snow-man of him.

All at once, as he stumbled on in the smothering darkness, his foot went down into a hole in the ground, and he fell, and there having once fallen, he found that he was too weak to rise, and it seemed to him that he would soon be nothing but a part of the snow, making a level, where there had been a hollow before.

Sleep began to creep under his cold eyelids, and he knew that it was the snow sleep that brings death.

The falling flakes grew black above him, no whiteness was to be seen anywhere; he felt them covering his face and growing heavy on his limbs, shutting him away from the things he had wished for or had loved. Never again could he hope to see life and the warm hearth of home or the delightful return of spring.

How long he lay there, letting thought go, forgetting everything, he could not tell; but when he came to himself again, he felt warmth at his breast, and opening his eyes, he found that a white hare had made her form in the snow over his heart.

His first thought was to lie quite still and be kept warm. "For if I move," thought he, "I shall scare her away and she will leave me to die." Yet after all would it not be quite easy for him with his quick hands to reach up and catch her unawares; then there would at least be one hare out of the ten for a beginning?

So he was thinking, when all at once a soft voice said to him; "Helnar, art thou awake?" It was the hare speaking.

Then Helnar, for he recognized the voice, that it was the same hare whose life he had spared before the snow began, returned answer: "O little friend," said he, "how came you here? Yes, in truth I find that I am awake, though I never thought to be again."

The white hare said, "Is it peace that brings you here, Helnar?"

"Nay," answered the youth. "It is war. For the snows have come down against us, burying our houses and our herds, and all the people are starving. And I have come to take tithe, that the Snowers may know that we are strong men, though we may be a small people."

"What is your tithe to be?" inquired the white hare.

"Little one," answered Helnar, "it has nothing to do with thee. We are friends; I have saved thy life, and thou hast saved mine. Between us it is peace."

"Can I let thee," said the white hare, "take ten other lives as dear to me as my own?"

"Little friend, you know too much," said Helnar. "How comes it?"

"Have I not warmed thy heart back to life?" said the white hare. "How then should I not know that its errand is cruelty."

"Nay," said Helnar, "this war came to us, not from us. It is only peace we seek, and room to live and breathe."

The white hare answered, "You can win peace peaceably, if you will only harken to me."

So then she told him what to do.

"Lie down," said she, "under this rock, and do not shake off the snow that now covers you. In a little while, you will see me return, and with me will be others. Then you have but to hold fast whatever I shall throw to you, and you will be safe. Only be sure that you do not let it go."

Then the white hare sprang up from his breast and disappeared; and Helnar lay and waited, all covered with snow except his face, till after a while he heard round about him the scurrying of feet; and there, making swift circles in the snow as it swirled and drifted, fifty white hare bucks came galloping; all as white as the ground on which they ran, so that when they sat down and stopped running they seemed to have vanished into the earth.

Presently, all but the white doe hare, leapt up together at a signal, and throwing off their hare-skins, appeared no longer to be hares at all, but fifty well-

dressed huntsmen, youthful and active. And as the thick snowflakes flew away before their breath, they danced like shuttles through a weaver's loom; and as they danced they shouted, stamping on the soft snow.

Thick and thicker fell the snow, in time to their dancing; then they all gave one stamp together and clapped hands, and drawing out made a wide circle, and so standing still, cried aloud as with one voice; "Moozi-poo! Come and dance to us while we rest."

Instantly, the white doe hare, that till then had sat apart, sprang up, and throwing off her skin coat, cast it toward Helnar, where he lay concealed under the snow, and went dancing like a snowflake in the moonbeams into the circle of her brethren.

But Helnar was so spellbound by her beauty and the strangeness of the thing that he could not reach out a hand even to take the hare-skin that had come warm off her fair body and now lay close beside him.

He could do nothing but watch and wonder, as she went dancing in and out, with the snowflakes flying like bees before her breath. For her dance was like the falling of may blossom before the breeze, or like spray on the crest of a shoreward wave, which the sun strikes, crowning it with a foam bow; or like a ring of white maidens spinning with linked arms—so fast she went with her dancing.

And as that dance went on, Helnar forgot to put out his hand and catch hold of the hare-skin.

Then, when she had ended, Moozipoo cried out to one of the huntsmen standing by; "Run, brother, and fetch

me my cloak which lies yonder." And as she spoke, she looked and saw it lying, and Helnar's hand not on it; so throwing up her arms she cried, "Quick! Quick!" for she was afraid that Helnar might be too late. At which the huntsman, thinking that she called to him, ran all the faster to get it and bring it for her.

But even as he came near, Helnar, freeing himself from the spell of her loveliness, only just in time put out his hand and caught the skin to his breast and held it.

Instantly the huntsman cried out in a lamentable loud voice: "Alas, sister, you are betrayed, and we are made desolate! For here is a man hidden under the snow, and he has hold of your hare-skin."

But Moozipoo cried back to him with light laughter, saying, "Foolish brother, why should any man want my hare-skin? Ask him for it, and he will give it you."

Then the young huntsman, coming to Helnar, spoke smoothly and cunningly, saying, "Stranger, I pray you give me back my sister's cloak, which you have in your hand there; for the night has grown cold, and she is in need of it."

But Helnar would not give it up.

Then said the maiden: "What, brother, art thou so churlish to a stranger? Offer him something in exchange as is seemly; then surely he will not refuse thee!"

So her brother, the huntsman, said to Helnar: "If thou art in need of anything, ask it of us, and we will grant the request; but let Moozipoo, my dear sister, have back her cloak, for you will see how cold she is without it."

But still Helnar would not give it up.

"Let her come for it herself," said he.

Then came Moozipoo, the fair maiden, and said to Helnar: "I pray you, kind stranger, let me have back my cloak, for this cold wind chills me to the marrow!"

Nevertheless, Helnar shut his eyes to her beauty and would not give it up.

Then she knelt and clasped her hands saying, "Have I done thee any unkindness that thou wilt not give me back my hare-skin?" Whereat Helnar, all distraught at her sweetness and her beauty and the distress of her speech, was almost minded to render the cloak up to her. But he remembered again what she had said to him in the first place and shut his ears to her entreaty.

Then Moozipoo's brethren, the well-clad huntsmen and warriors, each with his own hare-skin coat about him, gathered round watching their sister with looks of sad foreboding; and the maiden turned back to them saying, "Surely we know why he has come! Is it not ten white hare-skins that he is seeking? Which of you, my brothers, will give up what he holds most dear that I may go free?"

Then immediately, ten of the brethren laid down their hare-skins at Helnar's feet, saying, "Take!" But the youth had no longer an eye for the ten white hare-skins, which he had first come seeking. So they said: "What is it that you wish, stranger? Is it peace for the dwellers in the valleys who come into our hills setting traps? Is it peace you wish?"

And Helnar answered: "That, too, shall you give me; but what I wish most to have is this maiden whose cloak I now hold, that I may make her my wife, and bring her back with me to live among my own people."

Then said they all: "Alas, since thou hast asked this of us, we must grant it, for we cannot say "No" to him who has our sister's hare-skin in his keeping."

So, without more ado, they gave the maiden into his hand, and the ring with which, there and then, he was to wed her; which indeed he did gladly, having no other wish.

And each of her brethren coming in turn, laid his hare-skin cloak over her, saying, "Ah, dear sister, freely had I let mine be thine, but it avails not; for now the word is spoken, and thou, having found thy master, must go with him, even to the world's end."

But to Helnar they said: "Have a care and watch over and do no harm to Moozipoo, our dear sister, else shalt thou and thy people and all their village, be wiped off from the face of the earth!"

Then Helnar laid once more upon Moozipoo her own cloak of hare-skin, but she remained unchanged by it, looking at him with the eyes of love.

And at that all her brethren broke into sorry lamentations, crying: "Behold, now, Moozipoo, our sister, is already gone from us, and belongs to her tribe no more. Nor shall we ever again see her dance like falling blossoms and like snowflakes in the midst of our revels. Good-bye, Moozipoo. Yet do not throw away your hare-skin, so that you may always remember us and return

to us again if your heart changes."

Then each of the fifty brother huntsmen threw on their white hare-skin coats; and they all became hares once more and vanished away among the snow hollows into the heart of the hills, leaving the two lovers alone.

When Helnar, bringing his bride with him, came again within sight of his native village, the sun was already shining, the sky was blue, and the snow was beginning to melt on the roofs.

He brought her to his father's house and sat her down by the hearth in the seat of honor, saying to old Sveljik, "Here I have brought you a daughter, little father; and her dower is herself, that stands for ten white hare-skins, and peace to all the dwellers in the villages. Will you not bid her welcome to your roof?"

Then old Sveljik, being wise, rose up and gave her a father's welcome, blessing the peace which she had brought to them. But the brothers were envious and angry, saying: "Why should Helnar have a wife before we have, seeing that he is the youngest and the least of us? Only our eldest brother is married, and after his comes our turn." So they gave a cold welcome to Moozipoo, Helnar's wife, in spite of the peace she had brought with her. But more angry and jealous than all the rest was the eldest brother's wife; for she saw that old Sveljik, her father-in-law, would love Moozipoo better than he loved her, since Moozipoo was fairer of face and more beautiful of heart; also she had brought the spring weather two months before its time, so that for that year

there were two harvests, and all the people of the village lived in such plenty as they had never known till then.

So things went on, and Helnar and Moozipoo were as happy as only young married people can be; and when winter came round again, Moozipoo presented her husband with two of the most beautiful babes that had ever blessed the hopes of joyous wedlock. And the eldest brother's wife was now more angry and jealous than ever, for she had no child of her own; and now Moozipoo was far more honored than she was, even the brothers did not now complain against her.

Winter was well on, but the snow had not yet come; so one day Helnar said to his wife, "It cannot be long now before the snow comes; and when it falls, since it falls late, it is likely to remain long with us. So now that you are well and strong again, and I can leave you, I will go out hunting, that we may have a full larder when your brothers come to see us. Do not let the snow fall till I return."

Then Moozipoo kissed him and held up her two little ones that he might kiss them too, and Helnar set out, taking dogs and sleds and men with him, because he would be many days away and because they would surely have much to bring back with them.

And they went south toward the lake forests where the big game go for shelter for the winter.

But the night after he had gone, the eldest brother's wife rose up secretly and going to Moozipoo's bed where she lay asleep with her two little ones, she laid

hold of one of them and strangled the breath out of its body, so that when Moozipoo woke, there lay a babe dead under her right side.

And outside the world was all white with snow.

Then Moozipoo rose up weeping, and going to the closet where she kept her white hare-skin, she cut off one of its long white ears, and wrapped the child up in it and buried it in the snow outside the door of the house. And she sat all day with the other child upon her knee, saying nothing.

Old Sveljik, her father-in-law, said to her, "Where is the child that lies under your right side gone to?"

And Moozipoo answered, "It lies sick in its bed; do not trouble about it."

So old Sveljik said nothing more; and the eldest son's wife sat and looked on and wondered.

The next night she came again secretly, and going to Moozipoo's bed while she slept, she caught hold of the other child and squeezed the breath out of its body till there was none left. So in the morning when Moozipoo woke there lay a babe dead under her left side.

Then Moozipoo rose up weeping, and taking the white hare-skin, she cut off the second of its long white ears, and wrapping the child up in it, she buried it in the same place with the other one in the snow, which lay before the door of old Sveljik's house.

But this time, her sister-in-law had kept watch, and saw what she had done. So she went to her father-in-law, and said, "Do you know what Helnar's wife has done to her two children? She has killed them, and they

now lie buried in the snow that is outside the door. Question her, and see if she will tell you the truth."

So old Sveljik went in and found Moozipoo sitting by the hearth with her hands empty before her; and he said to her, "Where is the child that lies on your left side? Is it sick like the other one?"

And Moozipoo answered, "It lies sick in its bed along with its brother. Do not trouble about them."

Then old Sveljik was angry; and because he thought that she had lied to him, he believed all that his elder daughter-in-law had said. So he cried out to Moozipoo "You are a witch, and you have done wickedness, for you have killed your two children, though you have lived in my house for over a year and been treated as though you were my own daughter! Did I not love you enough, or did Helnar not love you enough, that you should do this thing the moment his back was turned? But now, since you have done it, you also shall die; and I cannot think of a death that is not too merciful, for surely burning is too good for one so evil!"

Then Moozipoo said, "Will you not wait till Helnar comes back? Surely if he condemn me, I will die gladly."

But her father-in-law said, "Helnar loved you too well; maybe he would beg for your evil life to be spared. Therefore you must die before he returns to save you from the reward of your wickedness."

Then Moozipoo said, "If I must die, bury me alive in the snow, by the bodies of my two little ones, for it is there they lie in the mound before the door. Can you wish me a more cruel death than that?"

So Sveljik, because that seemed indeed a cruel enough death, and because her body was too fair to be burned, took her at her word, and ordered the snow mound that lay before the door to be opened; and there when they dug, sure enough they found the two bodies of her little ones, each lying dead, wrapped in a cloak of white fur.

Then Moozipoo took her white hare-skin and wrapped herself in it from head to foot; and without resistance or lamentation she went out and was buried along with her two children in the snow mound which was before the door.

And when the snow was shoveled over her, the eldest son's wife went and trampled it down hard; and Sveljik and his sons and all the village folk came and walked over it, making it firm. That night, the sky like a black blanket came and lay down between the hills, and it began to snow.

Far away south, Helnar, looking toward home, saw that the snow had come and made haste to return.

"And why, then," thought he, "has Moozipoo forgotten her word to me, that she has let the snow come before I return? Surely if I do not make haste, there will not be food enough for our guests." So he pushed on until he came to where his native village should have been; and there, instead of its chimneys and roofs, he saw only a great snow mound.

When he beheld that and remembered what lay under, he thought not at all of old Sveljik, his father, nor of his brothers nor of his kinsmen, nor of the village folk; but he thought only of Moozipoo, his dear

wife whom he had left so happy with her two babes on her knees; and "Alas!" he cried, "what harm has come on thee, Moozipoo? Art thou dead, and is this the grave which the Snowers have made over thee?"

Then he saw upon the very top of the snow mound, a single white hare, like a sentinel keeping watch over all that solitude; and as soon as he was come near, Helnar cried to him, "Alas, white hare, if thou art one of the brethren, tell me, I pray thee, where is my dear wife, Moozipoo?"

Then the hare standing up on the mound answered in great wrath, "Dost thou, her husband, ask of me such a question? How hast thou watched over her and guarded her, whom it was thy promise to keep ever as the apple of thine eye from harm or shame? Ill shall it go with thee, since ill has happened to her; for surely she lies buried under this mound, slain by thy father and thy brethren and thy wicked sister-in-law; and her two little ones also lie slain with her. And had she not been faithful to thee in thought and deed, she might have come back to us; but now she lies here below, and we her brethren have built this grave over her. Thou, too, false brother, shalt find here a grave to cover thy shame and the treachery of all thy father's house!"

When Helnar heard that, he smote his hands together and answered not a word. But going up to the crest of the snow mound, he began digging with the broad blade of his hunting spear and shoveling out the snow with his hands, while the white hare sat and looked on.

All the night Helnar dug and uttered no sound. In the morning, the white hare looked down on him from above and said, "Thou art making thyself a deep grave, false brother!"

And Helnar looking up said, "Wait only until I have found what I seek for, brother, and then fill in my grave."

Ten days the white hare sat and watched while Helnar dug down into the heart of the snow mound. And now he was come lower than the roofs of the houses and was very near the thing he sought. On the tenth day, he came deep down upon the edge of a cloak made of white fur; and when he drew it open, there lay Moozipoo white and cold, with her two babes cuddled close in to her breast, each wrapped in its little cloak of hare-skin, like a bean in the velvety lining of its pod.

Then Helnar, beholding the goal of all his grief and his grave ready for him at last, stooped down and kissed his wife upon the lips, crying, "O Moozipoo, is there no room for me to lie by thy side?"

And hardly had he said this, when something quite wonderful happened; for Moozipoo opened her eyes and looked up softly out of sleep into her husband's face. And holding up the two children to be kissed also, she said, "O Helnar, be at peace, for I did but wait for thy return. There was slander told of me to thy father, and he believed it; and all thy brethren and the villagers believed it; little, therefore, are they to blame. And the only one who did not believe it was thy

brother's wife; for indeed the slander was all of her making. Now make haste, for here they all lie starving in their houses unable to get out; and let us call my brethren that may help us to make the snow mound disappear. But, alas, for thy sister-in-law when that is done, for they are fifty and she is one alone."

Then Helnar took his wife in his arms and his two children also and drew them up from the snow mound, wherein they had lain buried; and there upon the top stood ready the fifty brethren, the well-clad huntsmen and warriors, waiting to do Moozipoo's bidding, and after that to extend justice.

And when all was done, and old Sveljik and the rest of the starving folk had been rescued, there remained no more of the snow heap than was enough to bury Helnar's sister-in-law comfortably.

Then said Moozipoo to her husband as she unwound her cloak of white hare-skin, "Surely all this time, I have been faithful to thee in heart and thought and deed; for had I not been, I should have changed back into the form I came from and returned to my own people, to be seen of thee no more. But now, see, we have fifty brethren for our guests, and all thine own people are hungry also. Hast thou brought us a full larder, O Helnar, hunter of the white hare?"

SEVEN

The Cloak of Friendship

There was once upon a time a king who had two sons; and when he came to die did not know which of them it were best to leave his crown to, for though one was the elder, the other might be the fitter; and in that country the king alone had the right to say who should be king after him.

So as he lay dying, he bethought him of a way to prove them. Then he called his sons to him and said: "In a short while I shall be gone, and one of you must be king after me; which is it to be?" His sons remained in respectful silence, waiting on what they perceived he had yet to say to them; and, after observing them for a time thoughtfully, the king went on:

"Though you are equally dear to me as sons, yet I may not divide the kingdom between you to weaken

it; how then shall I know which of you will make the better ruler when I am gone? This is what I will do. I will show you all my secret treasures, and let each of you choose one of them: and the one that makes the best choice shall be king after me."

So the king led his sons into his treasury, and there showed them all his wealth and means of government; and especially he showed them the three chief treasures by which he maintained the strength and peace and security of his realm. The first was the Sword of Sharpness, whose property was to slay the king's enemies; there was no man so strong that he might stand against it. "It has won me my wars," said the king.

The second was the Cap of Darkness, whose property was to make the wearer of it invisible: by means thereof the king might go to and fro unperceived of any man and search out those that were in secret his enemies or plotters against the welfare of the state. "It has brought me to old age," said the king.

The third was the Cloak of Friendship. "It has brought me friends," said the king, "but its properties can only be learned by him who wears it; moreover, it is yet in the making and secures not all friendships, else would there be no wars and no plotters against the good estate of the realm. Now I have shown you my treasures, and it is for you to make choice."

Then the elder son spoke quick, saying: "The Sword of Sharpness! For with that, while I have life, I shall be strong and feared, being secure of victory." And he looked sharply at his younger brother, to whom also

"Make choice," said the king.

Then said the younger son: "My brother's choice deprives me of nothing that I wish for. Let the sword be his, and the crown with it. I choose the Cloak of Friendship."

The king said: "Your choice is the better one. After my death you shall be king."

So when the king died, his younger son, though still a child, was set upon the throne, while the elder, with the Sword of Sharpness, went to offer his services wherever war was, and to win fame; and great news of him came from all the countries around, while the young king sat in peace at home, with the Cloak of Friendship for his possession.

Now this cloak, of which the old king had told that it was yet a-making but not made, was fashioned in this wise: of every kind of animal in the world it contained one hair, and of every kind of bird under heaven it contained one feather; but it contained not the hair of a man. For whatever gave hair or feather to the weaving of that cloak must give life also, and freely, knowing the cost beforehand. Therefore was the cloak woven from the covering of all living kinds under heaven, saving of man; for no man would give his life freely to let one hair of his head carry with it the virtue of self-sacrifice to the weaving of the Cloak of Friendship.

Now when the old king gave the cloak to his son, he told him also its story: how a great wizard, learned in the speech of all living creatures upon earth, had in

the making of it spent a long lifetime. For going first to one and then to another of the tribes of feather and fur, he had said to each: "Find out one of you willing to die that he may have part in the Cloak of Friendship." Then they asked him: "What is this cloak, that we should die to have part in it?" And the wizard told them: "It is a cloak that will bring those that have share in it to be in friendship and understanding with man." And when they heard that, out of every tribe one was found ready to give up life for that friendship and understanding between them and man, which had been lost since Adam and Eve were driven out of Eden.

So the cloak came into making, but was not yet made, because as yet no man had been found to give up his life that through him with mankind the bond of friendship might be made whole. Even the wizard when he was dying would not give up one day of his life that its work might become accomplished. So had it been with the old king: "The less we have of life, little son," said he, "the more we cling to it. Thou art full of life, but do not die yet." And so saying he had laid upon the boy's shoulders the unfinished Cloak of Friendship.

The young king wearing the cloak felt the motions of its virtue within him and had a friendly eye for all living things; and of the lower kinds nothing feared him; he understood their speech and they his, nor were any of their ways strange to him. He knew why the starlings flock and are off again as at a word, and why the wild geese make always the same shape together in

flight, and why the dog turns three times in his kennel before he lies down, and why the fallow deer wags his tail before he lifts up his head from grass; and many things we have not the wits to see and hear that are common to all life, he saw and heard.

Thus he knew that on Christmas night, when the ox and the ass are talking in stall, there are others out and seeking to get word, while the Divine rumor runs between the earth and the stars, and to learn what the joy means of which the ox and the ass already know a little. But he knew also that it was well not to tell too much, else might the kind hearts of dumb things break with impatience for the relief which is surely one day to come, and with wonder at the hardness of men's hearts.

One Christmas night it was dark, though the ground was covered with snow; and the little king put on his cloak of feather and fur and stole out to the fields. And all around him in the air he felt the rumor of the Divine Birth moving to give rest to the hearts of men. Going where the track grew lost on the open down, he met a lame hare limping heavily over the snow.

"Gray hare, gray hare, where are you going so fast?" cried the young king.

And the hare answered: "Whither I go I know not, but danger is behind, and being lame I cannot go fast; yet it seemed to me that I should find shelter this night."

Then the king threw open his cloak and let it blow wide about his feet. "Come under the Cloak of Friendship," he said, "and you shall be safe."

And the hare limped under the hem of the king's cloak and cried: "There are multitudes of us here, yet I see none!"

"Wait and see!" said the king. So they went on.

Presently came a ferret running low on the scent of its prey. "Whither away, ferret?" said the king.

"To my supper," answered the ferret, "for I am cold and supperless, and tonight I smell good food ahead if I can only get to it."

"Turn in here," said the king, "and you shall have supper presently." And spreading his cloak wider, he let the ferret come under it.

"Good even to you, brother!" said the ferret, seeing the hare running close with him at the king's heels; and "Good even, brother!" said the hare. So together the three went on.

A little further and they met a fox; his thick tail brushed the snow as his feet sank in. "Red fox, red fox, where are you going tonight?" asked the king.

"Over the hill to the next farm," answered the fox. "There, under a rick, sleep three white geese, and I mean to have one of them, for tonight the farmer's dog has gone to a christening."

"What christening is that?" asked the king.

"Nay, I know not," answered the fox, "but I heard him today telling the shepherd's dog that tonight there was meat and a warm bed for them both, because of that christening feast. Thus I too profit," said the fox.

"Come under the Cloak of Friendship," said the king, "and you shall fare better than you think."

So the fox ran in alongside of the ferret and the hare, and they exchanged greetings all, and together went on.

"Here be three courses at least," said the fox, sniffing prophetic.

"And three mouths for the same," said the hare, quite as hungry as the rest.

Presently as they went further they met a wolf. "Wolf, wolf," said the king, "where are you going this night?"

"Over the hill, beyond the farm, to the fold," answered the wolf. "A good fat lamb is waiting for me there; and the shepherds will not see me tonight, for with good cheer and song they keep watch carelessly."

"Come under my cloak," said the king, "and you shall sup better with me."

So the wolf went in along with the others under the cloak, and "Merry company," cried he, seeing them all there, "luck be with us!" So they went on, and whatever they met by the way the king gathered under the Cloak of Friendship and led them on toward the farm. "For," thought he, "since I have saved the farmer a lamb and a goose, he may well feed us!"

There with his friendly rabble he knocked at the door. Out ran the farmer's dog and the sheepdog, barking; but the king had but to call them once, and they too came to heel like the rest.

"God shield us!" cried the farmer, all agape as he beheld the wolf and the fox and the ferret with all the

other beasts crowding behind. "What Noah's ark is this that is being loosed upon us now?"

"God be with you," said the young king.

"Amen!" said the farmer; "but for that get you gone!"

"Nay, we are hungry," said the king, "and tonight is peace on earth. Do not send all these away empty."

"Why should *I* feed them?" cried the farmer. "They steal food of me often enough; but tonight they bring their own meal with them: let them but look right and left! And as for you—let go my dogs; you are a wizard, I say. Out, out, else we will try fire on you!" And while some of those within caught up pitchforks, others drew out brands from the hearth and came running to the door to drive off such unwelcome applicants.

The king drew back from the threshold and let the door be closed. "Alas! little ones," said he to his friends, "I promised you food and warmth; yet now we must go further before we find it. Are you too cold or too hungry to come?"

"Nay, master," said the fox, "for under this cloak of yours I smell good meats ahead. We will yet come with you." And all the others said the same.

So the king turned back toward the city and brought them all under the Cloak of Friendship right up to the doors of the palace. Great was the astonishment of all there when they saw those strange guests. And the king ordered food and drink in abundance to be set before them: so they ate till they were filled; and after that the king sent them back in peace to their own homes,

promising in a year's time the same welcome to all who
would come.

On the morrow he noticed that people looked at him
strangely; they crooked their thumbs behind their backs
whenever his eye rested on them and seemed fearful of
coming near him. For, because of his strange guests of
the night before, all thought him a wizard, a dealer in
black magic even as the farmer had done. Then had he
bethought him of the Cap of Darkness which lay still
in the king's treasury, he could have learned much of
what was plotted behind his back; but his heart was full
of friendship for all men, and he thought not of such
means for guarding himself from danger.

So it was with joy that he heard soon after how his
brother was returning from all the wars that he had
been waging in other countries to visit once more the
realm of which he would have been king, had not his
brother's preferment ousted him.

"Ah, brother!" cried the young king, going out to
welcome him, "sheath your sword for a while and live
in peace with me; you have made wars too many and
stayed too long away from home."

The other answered him coldly: "Brother, long ago
your choice of peace seemed good to our father, when
he made you to be king: but my choice of the sword
seems good to me now. Strange friendship you seem
to have made; but your crown you must give up to me."

"Alas! brother," said the king, "has all your fame
left you room to be jealous of me and my office? Yet
it may well be that for a year you may wish to taste rule

over a peaceful kingdom. So, if you will, take mine; but let me keep still this Cloak of Friendship, which our father's own hands put on me before he died."

"You may keep it," said his brother; "but go not with it into strange places, nor do any more of the strange things you have done. Take heed, and let my word to you be law!"

So the elder brother took up the crown and ruled; and the other with little ado let it go and went his own way peacefully, coming and going with little notice from men. And of all his kingly appurtenances the Cloak of Friendship was now the only one that was left to him. That kept his heart warm and gave employment to his mind during the year that followed his deposition. But often he would look at the frayed edge, where it lacked finish because no man would give his life that the bond of friendship between man and beast might be made whole, and would wonder if ever it could be right for a man with a soul that lives to give up life for the sake of the beasts that perish.

So the year went round, and by no sign did the dethroned king show envy of the brother who had usurped his place; but often, beholding him, his heart grew sorrowful, for the Sword of Sharpness would not stay sheathed, and the land had no longer its former rest; and "Alas! brother," cried younger to elder, "now you make great wars: but when Christmas comes I will show you peace."

"What is peace?" inquired the other, scornfully.

"It is the Cloak of Friendship," he answered.

Now when Christmas was near, it was told to the elder brother how in his own house the younger was preparing a great feast without tables; and the tale of the Christmas before was revived. When the king heard of it, "Make no hindrance," said he, "but at the last bring me word, and my brother shall know which of us rules now and gives law."

On Christmas night, as soon as it was dark, the younger put on the Cloak of Friendship and set out to find his friends. And on the hillside he met them coming, for they all remembered his word to them, and with them they brought others, so that the ground was quick under them, and the snow dark with the trampling of their feet. To him came red deer and wild boar, fox and wolf, marten and stoat, polecat and badger, and with them also came the gentler and more timid kinds; and in greeting to them he said; "Peace be with you!" and spread the Cloak of Friendship wide that all might come under. So host and guests together turned and went back to the city. "This night," he said to them, "is the night of peace: fear no man!"

"What is peace?" asked the fox. "We know little thereof."

"It is the Cloak of Friendship," answered the young king. "Once it was so wide that it covered the whole world; but now it is shorn in pieces and shredded with age and rough usage, and only here and there can one find it. Nevertheless on this night, many years ago, He that wore it whole was born. So in memory of Him there is peace tonight through nature wherever goes under-

standing of Him. Come under the Cloak of Friendship with me, and you shall be filled."

Not long afterward word was brought to the elder brother in his palace that wizardry was at work once more and that the ways of the city swarmed with wild beasts, all going peaceably toward the feast that had been prepared without tables. "Let the city gates be shut," said the king, "and wait you for my word."

And straight upon that entered to him his brother, who kneeled to him and said: "Fair brother, tonight is the night of Christ's birth. Come with me, and I will show you peace."

"Nay, brother," answered the king coldly. "I have heard tell already of this brave hunting ground that you have prepared. So now, come with me and I will show you sport."

Quick with sudden fear the younger cried: "Brother, you will not kill?"

"As I choose," answered the other.

"Nay, for my honor is pledged to them! I have promised that they shall get no hurt."

"Make good thy promise!" said his brother, laughing; and, without more ado, he gave orders for the archers and the huntsmen with their hounds to make ready.

"Nay, nay, brother!" cried the other, distraught, "for if one of them is harmed I am dishonored forever."

"Thy dishonor is in making promises thou canst not perform," replied the king.

Whereat the other, speaking low and all heavy of

heart, answered: "Nay, brother, for what I promised that I will perform. Yet, since thus we must part, first give me the kiss of peace that afterward it may be known that there was love and not hate between us upon this night which is the joy of all Christian souls."

Then he took up the unfinished and frayed edge of the Cloak of Friendship and wove therein one hair of a man's head, even his own; and he stretched it wide, and drew it about his brother's shoulder, so that the same cloak enfolded both. And so standing in bond to his brother, he saw his face change and grow merciful and knew that the gift had been granted, so that he need fear no longer for the lives of the guests he had brought in with him for that night.

So he kissed him and said: "Fair brother, is it not peace?"

"Nay, what is peace?" cried the elder brother in sudden fear, beholding him so pale; and catching him in his arms he felt his flesh cold as a dead man's.

"It is the Cloak of Friendship," answered the young king; and straightway he kissed death, and his heart stopped from its work, having come to a good end.

EIGHT

The Prince with the Nine Sorrows

Eight white peahens went down to the gate:
"Wait!" they said, "little sister, wait!"
They covered her up with feathers so fine;
And none went out, when there went back nine.

A long time ago there lived a King and a **Queen,** who had an only son. As soon as he was born his mother gave him to the forester's wife to be nursed; for she herself had to wear her crown all day and had no time for nursing. The forester's wife had just given birth to a little daughter of her own; but she loved both children equally and nursed them together like twins.

One night the Queen had a dream that made the half of her hair turn gray. She dreamed that she saw the Prince her son at the age of twenty lying dead with

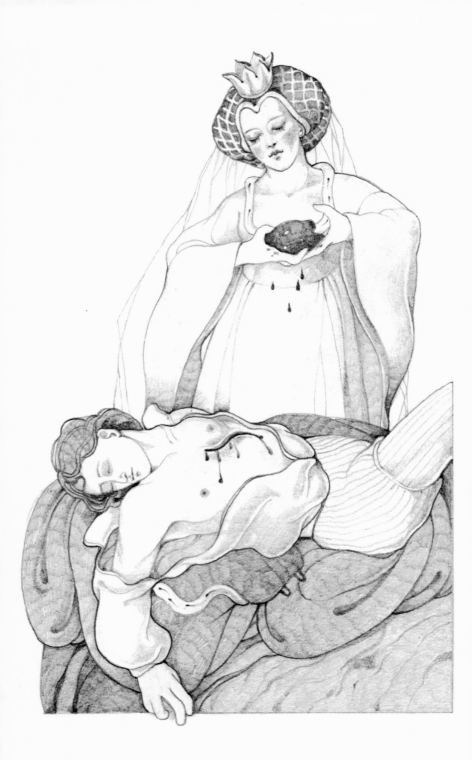

a wound over the place of his heart; and near him his foster-sister was standing, with a royal crown on her head, and his heart bleeding between her hands.

The next morning the Queen sent in great haste for the family Fairy and told her of the dream. The Fairy said, "This can have but one meaning, and it is an evil one. There is some danger that threatens your son's life in his twentieth year, and his foster-sister is to be the cause of it; also, it seems she is to make herself Queen. But leave her to me, and I will avert the evil chance; for the dream coming beforehand shows that the Fates mean that he should be saved."

The Queen said, "Do anything; only do not destroy the forester's wife's child, for, as yet at least, she has done no wrong. Let her only be carried away to a safe place and made secure and treated well. I will not have my son's happiness grow out of another one's grave."

The Fairy said, "Nothing is so safe as a grave when the Fates are about. Still, I think I can make everything quite safe within reason and leave you a clean as well as a quiet conscience."

The little Prince and the forester's daughter grew up together till they were a year old; then, one day, when their nurse came to look for them, the Prince was found, but his foster-sister was lost; and though the search for her was long, she was never seen again, nor could any trace of her be found.

The baby Prince pined and pined and was so sorrowful over her loss that they feared for a time that he was going to die. But his foster-mother in spite of her

grief over her own child's disappearance, nursed him so well and loved him so much that after a while he recovered his strength.

Then the forester's wife gave birth to another daughter, as if to console herself for the loss of the first. But the same night that the child was born the Queen had just the same dream over again. She dreamed that she saw her son lying dead at the age of twenty; and there was the wound in his breast, and the forester's daughter was standing by with his heart in her hand and a royal crown upon her head.

The poor Queen's hair had gone quite white when she sent again for the family Fairy and told her how the dream had repeated itself. The Fairy gave her the same advice as before, quieting her fears, and assuring her that however persistent the Fates might be in threatening the Prince's life, all in the end should be well.

Before another year was passed the second of the forester's daughters had disappeared; and the Prince and his foster-mother cried themselves ill over a loss that had been so cruelly renewed. The Queen, seeing how great were the sorrow and the love that the Prince bore for his foster-sisters, began to doubt in her heart and say, "What have I done? Have I saved my son's life by taking away his heart?"

Now every year the same thing took place, the forester's wife giving birth to a daughter and the Queen on the same night having the same fearful dream of the fate that threatened her son in his twentieth year;

and afterward the family Fairy would come, and then one day the forester's wife's child would disappear and be heard of no more.

At last when nine daughters in all had been born to the forester's wife and lost to her when they were but a year old, the Queen fell very ill. Every day she grew weaker and weaker, and the little Prince came and sat by her, holding her hand and looking at her with a sorrowful face. At last one night (it was just a year after the last of the forester's children had disappeared) she woke suddenly, stretching out her arms and crying. "Oh, Fairy," she cried, "the dream, the dream!" And covering her face with her hands, she died.

The little Prince was now more than ten years old, and the very saddest of mortals. He said that there were nine sorrows hidden in his heart, of which he could not get rid; and that at night, when all the birds went home to roost, he heard cries of lamentation and pain; but whether these came from very far away or out of his own heart, he could not tell.

Yet he grew slenderly and well and had such grace and tenderness in his nature that all who saw him loved him. His foster-mother, when he spoke to her of his nine sorrows, tried to comfort him, calling him her own nine joys; and, indeed, he was all the joy left in life for her.

When the Prince neared his twentieth year, the King his father felt that he himself was becoming old and weary of life. "I shall not live much longer," he thought: "very soon my son will be left alone in the world. It is

right, therefore, now that he should know of the danger ahead that threatens his life." For till then the Prince had not known anything; all had been kept a secret between the Queen and the King and the family Fairy.

The old King knew of the Prince's nine sorrows, and often he tried to believe that they came by chance and had nothing to do with the secret that sat at the root of his son's life. But now he feared more and more to tell the Prince the story of those nine dreams, lest the knowledge should indeed serve but as the crowning point of his sorrows and altogether break his heart for him.

Yet there was so much danger in leaving the thing untold that at last he summoned the Prince to his bedside, meaning to tell him all. The King had worn himself so ill with anxiety and grief in thinking over the matter, that now to tell all was the only means of saving his life.

The Prince came and knelt down and leaned his head on his father's pillow; and the King whispered into his ear the story of the dreams and of how for his sake all the Prince's foster-sisters had been spirited away.

Before his tale was done he could no longer bear to look into his son's face, but closed his eyes and, with long silences between, spoke as one who prayed.

When he had ended, he lay quite still, and the Prince kissed his closed eyelids and went softly out of the room.

"Now I know," he said to himself; "now at last!" And he came through the woods and knocked at his

foster-mother's door. "Other mother," he said to her, "give me a kiss for each of my sisters, for now I am going out into the world to find them, to be rid of the sorrows in my heart."

"They can never be found!" she cried, but she kissed him nine times. "And this," she said, "was Monica, and this was Ponica, and this was Veronica," and so she went over every name. "But now they are only names!" she wept, as she let him go.

He went along, and he went along, mile after mile. "Where may you be going to, fair sir?" asked an old peasant, at whose cabin the Prince sought shelter when night came to the first day of his wanderings. "Truly," answered the Prince, "I do not know how far or whither I need to go; but I have a fingerpost in my heart that keeps pointing me."

So that night he stayed there, and the next day he went on.

"Where to so fast?" asked a woodcutter when the second night found him in the thickest and loneliest parts of the forest. "Here the night is so dark and the way so dangerous, one like you should not go alone."

"Nay, I know nothing," said the Prince, "only I feel like a weathercock in a wind that keeps turning me to its will!"

After many days he came to a small long valley rich in woods and water-courses, but no road ran through it. More and more it seemed like the world's end, a place unknown or forgotten of its old inhabitants. Just at the end of the valley, where the woods opened

into clear slopes and hollows toward the west, he saw before him, low and overgrown, the walls of a little tumble-down grange. "There," he said to himself when he saw it, "I can find shelter for tonight. Never have I felt so tired before or such a pain at my heart!"

Before long he came to a little gate and a winding path that led in among lawns and trees to the door of an old house. The house seemed as if it had been once lived in, but there was no sign of any life about it now. He pushed open the door, and suddenly there was a sharp rustling of feathers, and nine white peahens rose up from the ground and flew out of the window into the garden.

The Prince searched the whole house over, and found it a mere ruin; the only signs of life to be seen were the white feathers that lifted and blew about over the floors.

Outside, the garden was gathering itself together in the dusk, and the peahens were stepping daintily about the lawns, picking here and there between the blades of grass. They seemed to suit the gentle sadness of the place, which had an air of grief that has grown at ease with itself.

The Prince went out into the garden, and walked about among the quietly stepping birds; but they took no heed of him. They came picking up their food between his very feet, as though he were not there. Silence held all the air, and in the cleft of the valley the day drooped to its end.

Just before it grew dark, the nine white peahens

gathered together at the foot of a great elm, and lifting up their throats, they wailed in chorus. Their lamentable cry touched the Prince's heart; "Where," he asked himself, "have I heard such sorrow before?" Then all with one accord the birds sprang rustling up to the lowest boughs of the elm and settled themselves to roost.

The Prince went back to the house to find some corner amid its half-ruined rooms to sleep in. But there the air was close, and an unpleasant smell of moisture came from the floor and walls: so, the night being warm, he returned to the garden and folding himself in his cloak, lay down under the tree where the nine peahens were at roost.

For a long time he tried to sleep but could not, there was so much pain and sorrow in his heart.

Presently when it was close upon midnight, over his head one of the birds stirred and ruffled through all its feathers; and he heard a soft voice say:

"Sisters, are you awake?"

All the other peahens lifted their heads and turned toward the one that had spoken, saying, "Yes, sister, we are awake."

Then the first one said again, "Our brother is here."

They all said, "He is our enemy; it is for him that we endure this sorrow."

"Tonight," said the first, "we may all be free."

They answered, "Yes, we may all be free! Who will go down and peck out his heart? Then shall be free."

And the first who had spoken said, "I will go down!"

"Do not fail, sister!" said all the others. "For if you fail, you can speak to us no more."

The first peahen answered, "Do not fear that I shall fail!" And she began stepping down the long boughs of the elm.

The Prince lying below heard all that was said. "Ah! poor sisters," he thought, "have I found you at last; and are all these sorrows brought upon you for me?" And he unloosed his doublet and opened his vest, making his breast bare for the peahen to come and pick out his heart.

He lay quite still with his eyes shut, and when she reached the ground, the peahen found him lying there, as it seemed to her fast asleep, with his white breast bare for the stroke of her beak.

Then so fair he looked to her and so gentle in his youth that she had pity on him and stood weeping by his side, and laying her head against his, whispered, "O, brother, once we lay as babes together and were nursed at the same breast! How can I peck out your heart?"

Then she stole softly back into the tree and crouched down again by her companions. They said to her, "Our minute of midnight is nearly gone. Is there blood on your beak! Have you our brother's heart for us?" But the other answered never a word.

In the morning the peahens came rustling down out of the elm and went searching for fat carnation buds and anemone seeds among the flower beds in

the garden. To the Prince they showed no sign either of hatred or fear but went to and fro carelessly, pecking at the ground about his feet. Only one came with drooping head and wings and sleeked itself to his caress, and the Prince, stooping down, whispered in her ear, "O, sister, why did you not peck out my heart?"

At night, as before, the peahens all cried in chorus as they went up into the elm; and the Prince came and wrapped himself in his cloak and lay down at the foot of it to watch.

At midnight the eight peahens lifted their heads and said, "Sister, why did you fail last night?" But their sister gave them not a word.

"Alas!" they said, "now she has failed, unless one of us succeed, we shall never hear her speak with her human voice again. Why is it that you weep so," they said again, "now when deliverance is so near?" For the poor peahen was shaken with weeping, and her tears fell down in loud drops upon the ground.

Then the next sister said, "I will go down! He is asleep. Be certain, I will not fail!" So she climbed softly down the tree, and the Prince opened his shirt and laid his breast bare for her to come and take out his heart.

Presently she stood by his side, and when she saw him, she too had pity on him for the youth and kindness of his face. And once she shut her eyes, and lifted her head for the stroke; but then weakness seized her, and she laid her head softly upon his heart and said, "Once the breast that gave me milk gave milk also to you. You were my sister's brother, and she spared you. How can

I peck out your heart?" And having said this, she went softly back into the tree and crouched down again among her sisters.

They said to her, "Have you blood upon your beak? Is his heart ours?" But she answered them no word.

The next day the two sisters, who because their hearts betrayed them had become mute, followed the Prince wherever he went and stretched up their heads to his caress. But the others went and came indifferently, careless except for food; for until midnight their human hearts were asleep; only now the two sisters who had given their voices away had regained their human hearts perpetually.

That night the same thing happened as before. "Sisters," said the youngest, "tonight I will go down, since the two eldest of us have failed. My wrong is fresher in my heart than theirs! Be sure I shall not fail!" So the youngest peahen came down from the tree, and the Prince laid his heart bare for her beak; but the bird could not find the will to peck it out. And so it was the next night, and the next, until eight nights were gone.

So at last only one peahen was left. At midnight she raised her head, saying, "Sisters, are you awake?"

They all turned and gazed at her, weeping, but could say no word.

Then she said, "You have all failed, having all tried but me. Now if I fail we shall remain mute and captive forever, more undone by the loss of our last remaining gift of speech than we were at first. But I tell you, dear

sisters, I will not fail; for the happiness of you all lies with me now!"

Then she went softly down the tree; and one by one they all went, following her and weeping, to see what the end would be.

They stood some way apart, watching with upturned heads, and their poor throats began catching back a wish to cry as the little peahen, the last of the sisters, came and stood by the Prince.

Then she, too, looked in his face and saw the white breast made bare for her beak; and the love of him went deep down into her heart. And she tried and tried to shut her eyes and deal the stroke but could not.

She trembled and sighed and turned to look at her sisters, where they all stood weeping silently together. "They have spared him," she said to herself: "why should not I?"

But the Prince, seeing that she, too, was about to fail like the rest of them, turned and said, as if in his sleep, "Come, come, little peahen, and peck out my heart!"

At that she turned back again to him and laid her head down upon his heart and cried more sadly than them all.

Then he said, "You have eight sisters and a mother who cries for her children to return!" Yet still she thought he was dreaming, and speaking only in his sleep. The other peahens came no nearer, but stood weeping silently. She looked from him to them. "O," she cried, "I have a wicked heart, to let one stand in the

way of nine!" Then she threw up her neck and cried lamentably with her peafowl's voice, wishing that the Prince would wake up and see her and so escape. And at that all the other peahens lifted up their heads and wailed with her: but the Prince never turned nor lifted a finger nor uttered a sound.

Then she drew in a deep breath and closed her eyes fast. "Let my sister go, but let me be as I am!" she cried; and with that she stooped down, and pecked out his heart.

All her sisters shrieked as their human shapes returned to them. "O, sister! O, wicked little sister!" they cried, "What have you done?"

The little white peahen crouched close down to the side of the dead Prince. "I loved him more than you all!" she tried to say: but she only lifted her head and wailed again and again the peafowl's cry.

The Prince's heart lay beating at her feet, so glad to be rid of its nine sorrows that mere joy made it live on, though all the rest of the body lay cold.

The peahen leaned down upon the Prince's breast, and there wailed without ceasing: then suddenly, piercing with her beak her own breast, she drew out her own living heart and laid it in the place where his had been.

And, as she did so, the wound where she had pierced him closed and became healed; and her heart was, as it were, buried in the Prince's breast. In her death agony she could feel it there, her own heart leaping within his breast for joy.

The Prince, who had seemed to be dead, flushed

from head to foot as the warmth of life came back to him; with one deep breath he woke and found the little white peahen lying as if dead between his arms.

Then he laughed softly and rose (his goodness making him wise), and taking up his own still beating heart he laid it into the place of hers. At the first beat of it within her breast, the peahen became transformed as all her sisters had been, and her own human form came back to her. And the pain and the wound in her breast grew healed together, so that she stood up alive and well in the Prince's arms.

"Dear heart!" said he: and "Dear, dear heart!" said she; but whether they were speaking of their own hearts or of each other's, who can tell? for which was which they themselves did not know.

Then all around was so much embracing and happiness that it is out of reach for tongue or pen to describe. For truly the Prince and his foster-sisters loved each other well and could put no bounds upon their present contentment. As for the Prince and the one who had plucked out his heart, of no two was the saying ever more truly told that they had lost their hearts to each other; nor was ever love in the world known before that carried with it such harmony as theirs.

And so it all came about according to the Queen's dream that the forester's daughter wore the royal crown upon her head and held the Prince's heart in her hand.

Long before he died the old King was made happy because the dream he had so much feared had become

true. And the forester's wife was happy before she died. And as for the Prince and his wife and his foster-sisters, they were all rather happy; and none of them is dead yet.

NINE

The White Doe

One day, as the king's huntsman was riding in the forest, he came to a small pool. Fallen leaves covering its surface had given it the color of blood, and knee-deep in their midst stood a milk-white doe drinking.

The beauty of the doe set fire to the huntsman's soul; he took an arrow and aimed well at the wild heart of the creature. But as he was loosing the string, the branch of a tree overhanging the pool struck him across the face and caught hold of him by the hair; and arrow and doe vanished away together into the depths of the forest.

Never until now, since he entered the king's service, had the huntsman missed his aim. The thought of the white doe living after he had willed its death inflamed him with rage; he could not rest till he had brought

hounds to the trail, determined to follow until it had surrendered to him its life.

All day, while he hunted, the woods stayed breathless, as if to watch; not a blade moved, not a leaf fell. About noon a red deer crossed his path; but he paid no heed, keeping his hounds only to the white doe's trail.

At sunset a fallow deer came to disturb the scent, and through the twilight, as it deepened, a gray wolf ran in and out of the underwood. When night came down, his hounds fled from his call, following through tangled thickets a huge black boar with crescent tusks. So he found himself alone, with his horse so weary that it could scarcely move.

But still, though the moon was slow in its rising, the fever of the chase burned in the huntsman's veins, and caused him to press on. For now he found himself at the rocky entrance of a ravine whence no way led; and the white doe being still before him, he made sure that he would get her at last. So when his horse fell, too tired to rise again, he dismounted and forced his way on; and soon he saw before him the white doe, laboring up an ascent of sharp crags, while closer and higher the rocks rose and narrowed on every side. Presently she had leaped high upon a boulder that shook and swayed as her feet rested, and ahead the wall of rocks had joined so that there was nowhere farther that she might go.

Then the huntsman notched an arrow and drew with full strength and let it go. Fast and straight it went,

and the wind screamed in the red feathers as they flew; but faster the doe overleaped his aim, and, spurning the stone beneath, down the rough-bouldered gully sent it thundering, shivering to fragments as it fell. Scarcely might the huntsman escape death as the great mass swept past: but when the danger was over, he looked ahead and saw plainly, where the stone had once stood, a narrow opening in the rock and a clear gleam of moonlight beyond.

That way he went and, passing through, came upon a green field, as full of flowers as a garden, duskily shining now and with dark shadows in all its folds. Around it in a great circle the rocks made a high wall, so high that along their crest forest trees as they clung to look over seemed but as low-growing thickets against the sky.

The huntsman's feet stumbled in shadow and trod through thick grass into a quick-flowing streamlet that ran through the narrow way by which he had entered. He threw himself down into its cool bed and drank till he could drink no more. When he rose he saw, a little way off, a small dwelling house of rough stone, moss covered and cozy, with a roof of wattles, which had taken root and pushed small shoots and clusters of gray leaves through their weaving. Nature, and not man, seemed there to have been building herself an abode.

Before the doorway ran the stream, a track of white mist showing where it wound over the meadow; and by its edge a beautiful maiden sat and was washing

her milk-white feet and arms in the wrinkling eddies.

To the huntsman she became all at once the most beautiful thing that the world contained; all the spirit of the chase seemed to be in her blood, and each little movement of her feet made his heart pump for joy. "I have looked for you all my life!" thought he, as he halted and gazed, not daring to speak lest the lovely vision should vanish, and the memory of it mock him forever.

The beautiful maiden looked up from her washing. "Why have you come here?" said she.

The huntsman answered her as he believed to be the truth, "I have come because I love you!"

"No," she said, "you came because you wanted to kill the white doe. If you wish to kill her, it is not likely that you can love me."

"I do not wish to kill the white doe!" cried the huntsman; "I had not seen you when I wished that. If you do not believe that I love you, take my bow and shoot me to the heart; for I will never go away from you now."

At his word she took one of the arrows, looking curiously at the red feathers, and to test the sharp point she pressed it against her breast. "Have a care!" cried the hunter, snatching it back. He drew his breath sharply and stared. "It is strange," he declared; "a moment ago I almost thought that I saw the white doe."

"If you stay here tonight," said the maiden, "about midnight you will see the white doe go by. Take this arrow and have your bow ready and watch! And if

tomorrow, when I return, the arrow is still unused in your hand, I will believe you when you say that you love me. And you have only to ask, and I will do all that you desire."

Then she gave the huntsman food and drink and a bed of ferns upon which to rest. "Sleep or wake," said she as she parted from him; "if truly you have no wish to kill the white doe, why should you wake? Sleep!"

"I do not wish to kill the white doe," said the huntsman. Yet he could not sleep: the memory of the one wild creature, which had escaped him, stung his blood. He looked at the arrow, which he held ready and grew thirsty at the sight of it. "If I see, I must shoot!" cried his hunter's heart. "If I see, I must not shoot!" cried his soul, smitten with love for the beautiful maiden and remembering her word. "Yet, if I see, I know I must shoot—so shall I lose all!" he cried as midnight approached, and the fever of long waiting remained unassuaged.

Then with a sudden will he drew out his hunting knife, and scored the palms of his two hands so deeply that he could no longer hold his bow or draw the arrow upon the string. "Oh, fair one, I have kept my word to you!" he cried as midnight came. "The bow and the arrow are both ready."

Looking forth from the threshold by which he lay, he saw pale moonlight and mist making a white haze together on the outer air. The white doe ran by, a body of silver; like quicksilver she ran. And the huntsman, the passion to slay rousing his blood, caught up arrow

and bow and tried in vain with his maimed hands to notch the shaft upon the string.

The beautiful creature leaped lightly by, between the curtains of moonbeam and mist; and as she went she sprang this way and that across the narrow streamlet, till the pale shadows hid her altogether from his sight. "Ah! ah!" cried the huntsman, "I would have given all my life to be able to shoot then! I am the most miserable man alive; but tomorrow I will be the happiest. What a thing is love, that it has known how to conquer in me even my hunter's blood!"

In the morning the beautiful maiden returned; she came sadly. "I gave you my word," said she: "here I am. If you have the arrow still with you as it was last night, I will be your wife, because you have done what never huntsman before was able to do—not to shoot at the white doe when it went by."

The huntsman showed her the unused arrow; her beauty made him altogether happy. He caught her in his arms and kissed her till the sun grew high. Then she brought food and set it before him; and taking his hand, "I am your wife," said she, "and with all my heart my will is to serve you faithfully. Only, if you value your happiness, do not shoot ever at the white doe." Then she saw that there was blood on his hand, and her face grew troubled. She saw how the other hand also was wounded. "How came this?" she asked; "dear husband, you were not so hurt yesterday."

And the huntsman answered, "I did it for fear lest

in the night I should fail and shoot at the white doe when it came."

Hearing that, his wife trembled and grew white. "You have tricked us both," she said, "and have not truly mastered your desire. Now, if you do not promise me on your life and your soul, or whatever is dearer, never to shoot at a white doe, sorrow will surely come of it. Promise me, and you shall certainly be happy!"

So the huntsman promised faithfully, saying, "On your life, which is dearer to me than my own, I give you my word to keep that it shall be so." Then she kissed him and bound up his wounds with healing herbs; and to look at her all that day, and for many days after, was better to him than all the hunting the king's forest could provide.

For a whole year they lived together in perfect happiness, and two children came to bless their union —a boy and a girl born at the same hour. When they were but a month old they could run; and to see them leaping and playing before the door of their home made the huntsman's heart jump for joy. "They are forest-born, and they come of a hunter's blood; that is why they run so early, and have such limbs," said he.

"Yes," answered his wife, "that is partly why. When they grow older they will run so fast—do not mistake them for deer if ever you go hunting."

No sooner had she said the word than the memory of it, which had slept for a whole year, stirred his blood. The scent of the forest blew up through the rocky

ravine, which he had never repassed since the day when he entered, and he laid his hands thoughtfully on the weapons he no longer used.

Such restlessness took hold of him all that day that at night he slept ill and, waking, found himself alone with no wife at his side. Gazing about the room, he saw that the cradle also was empty. "Why," he wondered, "have they gone out together in the middle of the night?"

Yet he gave it little more thought, and turning over, fell into a troubled sleep and dreamed of hunting and of the white doe that he had seen a year before stooping to drink among the red leaves that covered the forest pool.

In the morning his wife was by his side, and the little ones lay asleep upon their crib. "Where were you," he asked, "last night? I woke, and you were not here."

His wife looked at him tenderly, and sighed. "You should shut your eyes better," said she. "I went out to see the white doe, and the little ones came also. Once a year I see her; it is a thing I must not miss."

The beauty of the white doe was like strong drink to his memory: the beautiful limbs that had leaped so fast and escaped—they alone, of all the wild life in the world, had conquered him. "Ah!" he cried, "let me see her, too; let her come tame to my hand, and I will not hurt her!"

His wife answered: "The heart of the white doe is too wild a thing; she cannot come tame to the hand of

any hunter under heaven. Sleep again, dear husband, and wake well! For a whole year you have been sufficiently happy; the white doe would only wound you again in your two hands."

When his wife was not by, the hunter took the two children upon his knee, and said, "Tell me, what was the white doe like? what did she do? and what way did she go?"

The children sprang off his knee and leaped to and fro over the stream. "She was like this," they cried, "and she did this, and this was the way she went!" At that the hunter drew his hand over his brow. "Ah," he said, "I seemed then almost to see the white doe."

Little peace had he from that day. Whenever his wife was not there, he would call the little ones to him and cry, "Show me the white doe and what she did." And the children would leap and spring this way and that over the little stream before the door, crying, "She was like this, and she did this, and this was the way she went!"

The huntsman loved his wife and children with a deep affection, yet he began to have a dread that there was something hidden from his eyes, which he wished yet feared to know. "Tell me," he cried one day, half in wrath, when the fever of the white doe burned more than ever in his blood, "tell me where the white doe lives, and why she comes, and when next. For this time I must see her, or I shall die of the longing that has hold of me!" Then, when his wife would give no answer,

he seized his bow and arrows and rushed out into the forest, which for a whole year had not known him, slaying all the red deer he could find.

Many he slew in his passion, but he brought none of them home, for before the end a strange discovery came to him, and he stood amazed, dropping the haunch which he had cut from his last victim. "It is a whole year," he said to himself, "that I have not tasted meat; I, a hunter, who love only the meat that I kill!"

Returning home late, he found his wife troubling her heart over his long absence. "Where have you been?" she asked him, and the question inflamed him into a fresh passion.

"I have been out hunting for the white doe," he cried; "and she carries a spot in her side where some day my arrow must enter. If I do not find her, I shall die!"

His wife looked at him long and sorrowfully; then she said: "On your life and soul be it, and on mine also, that your anger makes me tell what I would have kept hidden. It is tonight that she comes. Now it remains for you to remember your word once given to me!

"Give it back to me!" he cried; "it is my fate to finish the quest of the white doe."

"If I give it," said she, "your happiness goes with it, and mine, and that of our children."

"Give it back to me!" he said again; "I cannot live unless I may master the white doe! If she will come tame to my hand, no harm shall happen to her."

And when she denied him again, he gave her his bow and arrows and bade her shoot him to the heart,

since without his word rendered back to him he could not live.

Then his wife took both his hands and kissed them tenderly and with loud weeping quickly set him free of his promise. "As well," said she, "ask the hunter to go bound to the lion's den as the white doe to come tame into your keeping; though she loved you with all her heart, you could not look at her and not be her enemy." She gazed on him with full affection and sighed deeply. "Lie down for a little," she said, "and rest; it is not till midnight that she comes. When she comes, I will wake you."

She took his head in her hands and set it upon her knee, making him lie down. "If she will come and stand tame to my hand," he said again, "then I will do her no harm."

After a while he fell asleep; and, dreaming of the white doe, started awake to find it was already midnight, and the white doe standing there before him. But as soon as his eyes lighted on her, they kindled with such fierce ardor that she trembled and sprang away out of the door and across the stream. "Ah, ah, white doe, white doe!" cried the wind in the feathers of the shaft that flew after her.

Just at her leaping of the stream, the arrow touched her; and all her body seemed to become a mist that dissolved and floated away, broken into thin fragments over the fast-flowing stream.

By the hunter's side his wife lay dead, with an arrow struck into her heart. The door of the house was shut;

it seemed to be only an evil dream from which he had suddenly awakened. But the arrow gave real substance to his hand: when he drew it out, a few true drops of blood flowed after. Suddenly the hunter knew all he had done. "Oh, white doe, white doe!" he cried, and fell down with his face to hers.

At the first light of dawn he covered her with dry ferns that the children might not see how she lay there dead. "Run out," he cried to them, "run out and play! Play as the white doe used to do!" And the children ran out and leaped this way and that across the stream, crying, "She was like this, and she did this, and this was the way she went!"

So while they played along the banks of the stream, the hunter took up his beautiful dead wife and buried her. And to the children he said, "Your mother has gone away; when the white doe comes, she will return also."

"She was like this," they cried, laughing and playing, "and she did this, and this was the way she went!" And all the time as they played, he seemed to see the white doe leaping before him in the sunlight.

That night the hunter lay sleepless on his bed, wishing for the world to end; but in the crib by his side the two children lay in a sound slumber. Then he saw plainly in the moonlight, the white doe with a red mark in her side, standing still by the doorway. Soon she went to where the young ones were lying, and as she touched the coverlet softly with her right forefoot, all at once two young fawns rose up from the ground

and sprang away into the open, following where the white doe beckoned them.

Nor did they ever return. For the rest of his life the huntsman stayed where they left him, a sorrowful and lonely man. In the grave where lay the woman's form he had slain, he buried his bow and arrows far from the sight of the sun or the reach of his own hand; and coming to the place night by night, he would watch the mists and the moonrise and cry, "White doe, white doe, will you not some day forgive me?" and did not know that she had forgiven him then when, before she died, she kissed his two hands and made him sleep for the last time with his head on her knee.

TEN

A Chinese Fairy Tale

Tiki-pu was a small grub of a thing; but he had a true love of Art deep down in his soul. There it hung mewing and complaining, struggling to work its way out through the raw exterior that bound it.

Tiki-pu's master professed to be an artist: he had apprentices and students, who came daily to work under him, and a large studio littered about with the performances of himself and his pupils. On the walls hung also a few real works by the older men, all long since dead.

This studio Tiki-pu swept; for those who worked in it, he ground colors, washed brushes, and ran errands, bringing them their dog chops and bird's nest soup from the nearest eating house whenever they were too busy to go out to it themselves. He himself had to feed

mainly on the breadcrumbs, which the students screwed into pellets for their drawings and then threw about upon the floor. It was on the floor, also, that he had to sleep at night.

Tiki-pu looked after the blinds and mended the paper windowpanes, which were often broken when the apprentices threw their brushes and maulsticks at him. Also he strained rice paper over the linen stretchers, ready for the painters to work on; and for a treat, now and then, a lazy one would allow him to mix a color for him. Then it was that Tiki-pu's soul came down into his fingertips, and his heart beat so that he gasped for joy. Oh, the yellows and the greens, and the lakes and the cobalts, and the purples which sprang from the blending of them! Sometimes it was all he could do to keep himself from crying out.

Tiki-pu, while he squatted and ground at the color powders, would listen to his master lecturing to the students. He knew by heart the names of all the painters and their schools and the name of the great leader of them all who had lived and passed from their midst more than three hundred years ago; he knew that too, a name like the sound of the wind, Wio-wani: the big picture at the end of the studio was by him.

That picture! To Tiki-pu it seemed worth all the rest of the world put together, He knew, too, the story which was told of it, making it as holy to his eyes as the tombs of his own ancestors. The apprentices joked over it, calling it "Wio-wani's back door," "Wio-wani's nightcap," and many other nicknames; but Tiki-pu

was quite sure, since the picture was so beautiful, that the story must be true.

Wio-wani, at the end of a long life, had painted it; a garden full of trees and sunlight, with high-standing flowers and green paths, and in their midst a palace. "The place where I would like to rest," said Wio-wani, when it was finished.

So beautiful was it then, that the Emperor himself had come to see it; and gazing enviously at those peaceful walks and the palace nestling among the trees, had sighed and owned that he too would be glad of such a resting-place. Then Wio-wani stepped into the picture and walked away along a path till he came, looking quite small and far off, to a low door in the palace wall. Opening it, he turned and beckoned to the Emperor; but the Emperor did not follow; so Wio-wani went in by himself and shut the door between himself and the world forever.

That happened three hundred years ago; but for Tiki-pu the story was as fresh and true as if it had happened yesterday. When he was left to himself in the studio, all alone and locked up for the night, Tiki-pu used to go and stare at the picture till it was too dark to see and at the little palace with the door in its wall by which Wio-wani had disappeared out of life. Then his soul would go down into his fingertips, and he would knock softly and fearfully at the beautifully painted door, saying, "Wio-wani, are you there?"

Little by little in the long thinking nights and the slow early mornings when lights began to creep back

through the papered windows of the studio, Tiki-pu's soul became too much for him. He who could strain paper and grind colors and wash brushes had everything within reach for becoming an artist, if it was the will of Fate that he should be one.

He began timidly at first, but in a little while he grew bold. With the first wash of light he was up from his couch on the hard floor and was daubing his soul out on scraps and odds and ends and stolen pieces of rice paper.

Before long the short spell of daylight, which lay between dawn and the arrival of the apprentices to their work, did not suffice him. It took him so long to hide all traces of his doings, to wash out the brushes and rinse clean the paintpots he had used, and on the top of that to get the studio swept and dusted, that there was hardly time left him in which to indulge the itching of his fingers.

Driven by necessity, he became a pilferer of candle ends, picking them from their sockets in the lanterns, which the students carried on dark nights. Now and then one of these would remember that, when last used, his lantern had had a candle in it, and would accuse Tiki-pu of having stolen it. "It is true," he would confess; "I was hungry—I have eaten it." The lie was so probable, he was believed easily and was well beaten accordingly. Down in the ragged linings of his coat Tiki-pu could hear the candle ends rattling as the buffeting and chastisement fell upon him, and often he trembled lest his hoard should be discovered. But the

truth of the matter never leaked out; and at night, as soon as he guessed that all the world outside was in bed, Tiki-pu would mount one of his candles on a wooden stand and paint by the light of it, blinding himself over his task, till the dawn came and gave him a better and cheaper light to work by.

Tiki-pu quite hugged himself over the results; he believed he was doing very well. "If only Wio-wani were here to teach me," thought he, "I would be in the way to becoming a great painter!"

The resolution came to him one night that Wio-wani *should* teach him. So he took a large piece of rice paper and strained it, and sitting down opposite "Wio-wani's back door," began painting. He had never set himself so big a task as this; by the dim stumbling light of his candle he strained his eyes nearly blind over the difficulties of it; and at last was almost driven to despair. How the trees stood row behind row, with air and sunlight between, and how the path went in and out, winding its way up to the little door in the palace wall were mysteries he could not fathom. He peered and peered and dropped tears into his paintpots; but the secret of the mystery of such painting was far beyond him.

The door in the palace wall opened; out came a little old man and began walking down the pathway toward him.

The soul of Tiki-pu gave a sharp leap in his grubby little body. "That must be Wio-wani himself and no other!" cried his soul.

Tiki-pu pulled off his cap and threw himself down on the floor with reverent grovelings. When he dared to look up again, Wio-wani stood over him big and fine; just within the edge of his canvas he stood and reached out a hand.

"Come along with me, Tiki-pu!" said the great one. "If you want to know how to paint, I will teach you."

"Oh, Wio-wani, were you there all the while?" cried Tiki-pu ecstatically, leaping up and clutching with his smeary little puds the hand, which the old man extended to him.

"I was there," said Wio-wani, "looking at you out of my little window. Come along in!"

Tiki-pu took a heave and swung himself into the picture and fairly capered when he found his feet among the flowers of Wio-wani's beautiful garden. Wio-wani had turned and was ambling gently back to the door of his palace, beckoning to the small one to follow him; and there stood Tiki-pu, opening his mouth like a fish to all the wonders that surrounded him. "Celestiality, may I speak?" he said suddenly.

"Speak," replied Wio-wani; "what is it?"

"The Emperor, was he not the very flower of fools not to follow when you told him?"

"I cannot say," answered Wio-wani, "but he certainly was no artist."

Then he opened the door, that door which he had so beautifully painted, and led Tiki-pu in. And outside the little candle end sat and guttered by itself, till the wick fell overboard, and the flame kicked itself

out, leaving the studio in darkness and solitude to wait for the growings of another dawn.

It was full day before Tiki-pu reappeared; he came running down the green path in great haste, jumped out of the frame onto the studio floor, and began tidying up his own messes of the night and the apprentices' of the previous day. Only just in time did he have things ready by the hour when his master and the others returned to their work.

All that day they kept scratching their left ears and could not think why; but Tiki-pu knew, for he was saying over to himself all the things that Wio-wani, the great painter, had been saying about them and their precious productions. And as he ground their colors for them and washed their brushes and filled his famished little body with the breadcrumbs they threw away, little they guessed from what an immeasurable distance he looked down upon them all and had Wio-wani's word for it tickling his right ear all the day long.

Now before long Tiki-pu's master noticed a change in him; and though he bullied him and thrashed him and did all that a careful master should do, he could not get the change out of him. So in a short while he grew suspicious. "What is the boy up to?" he wondered. "I have my eye on him all day: it must be at night that he gets into mischief."

It did not take Tiki-pu's master a night's watching to find that something surreptitious was certainly going on. When it was dark, he took up his post outside the studio, to see whether by any chance Tiki-pu had some

way of getting out; and before long he saw a faint light showing through the window. So he came and thrust his finger softly through one of the panes and put his eye to the hole.

There inside was a candle burning on a stand and Tiki-pu squatting with paintpots and brush in front of Wio-wani's last masterpiece.

"What fine piece of burglary is this?" thought he; "what serpent have I been harboring in my bosom? Is this beast of a grub of a boy thinking to make himself a painter and cut me out of my reputation and prosperity?" For even at that distance he could perceive plainly that the work of this boy went head and shoulders beyond his or that of any painter then living.

Presently Wio-wani opened his door and came down the path, as was his habit now each night, to call Tiki-pu to his lesson. He advanced to the front of his picture and beckoned for Tiki-pu to come in with him; and Tiki-pu's master grew clammy at the knees as he beheld Tiki-pu catch hold of Wio-wani's hand and jump into the picture and skip up the green path by Wio-wani's side and in through the little door that Wio-wani had painted so beautifully in the end wall of his palace!

For a time Tiki-pu's master stood glued to the spot with grief and horror. "Oh, you deadly little underling! Oh, you poisonous little caretaker, you parasite, you vampire, you fly in amber!" cried he. "Is that where you get your training? Is it there that you dare to go trespassing; into a picture that I purchased for my own

pleasure and profit, and not at all for yours? Very soon we will see whom it really belongs to!"

He ripped out the paper of the largest window pane and pushed his way through into the studio. Then in great haste he took up paintpot and brush and sacrilegiously set himself to work upon Wio-wani's last masterpiece. In the place of the doorway by which Tiki-pu had entered, he painted a solid brick wall; twice over he painted it, making it two bricks thick; brick by brick he painted it and mortared every brick to its place. And when he had quite finished he laughed and called, "Good night, Tiki-pu!" and went home to be quite happy.

The next day all the apprentices were wondering what had become of Tiki-pu; but as the master himself said nothing and as another boy came to act as color grinder and brush washer to the establishment, they very soon forgot all about him.

In the studio the master used to sit at work with his students all about him and a mind full of ease and contentment. Now and then he would throw a glance across to the bricked-up doorway of Wio-wani's palace and laugh to himself, thinking how well he had served out Tiki-pu for his treachery and presumption.

One day—it was five years after the disappearance of Tiki-pu—he was giving his apprentices a lecture on the glories and the beauties and the wonders of Wio-wani's painting—how nothing for color could excel, or for mystery could equal it. To add point to his elo-

quence, he stood waving his hands before Wio-wani's last masterpiece, and all his students and apprentices sat around him and looked.

Suddenly he stopped at mid-word and broke off in the full flight of his eloquence, as he saw something like a hand come and take down the top brick from the face of paint which he had laid over the little door in the palace wall, which Wio-wani had so beautifully painted. In another moment there was no doubt about it; brick by brick the wall was being pulled down, in spite of its double thickness.

The lecturer was altogether too dumbfounded and terrified to utter a word. He and all his apprentices stood around and stared while the demolition of the wall proceeded. Before long he recognized Wio-wani with his flowing white beard; it was his handiwork, this pulling down of the wall! He still had a brick in his hand when he stepped through the opening that he had made, and close after him stepped Tiki-pu!

Tiki-pu was grown tall and strong—he was even handsome; but for all that his old master recognized him and saw with an envious foreboding that under his arms he carried many rolls and stretchers and portfolios and other belongings of his craft. Clearly Tiki-pu was coming back into the world and was going to be a great painter.

Down the garden path came Wio-wani, and Tiki-pu walked after him; Tiki-pu was so tall that his head stood well over Wio-wani's shoulders—old man and young man together made a handsome pair.

How big Wio-wani grew as he walked down the avenues of his garden and into the foreground of his picture! And how big the brick in his hand! And ah, how angry he seemed!

Wio-wani came right down to the edge of the picture frame and held up the brick. "What did you do that for?" he asked.

"I . . . didn't!" Tiki-pu's old master was beginning to reply; and the lie was still rolling on his tongue when the weight of the brickbat, hurled by the stout arm of Wio-wani, felled him. After that he never spoke again. That brickbat, which he himself had reared, became his own tombstone.

Just inside the picture frame stood Tiki-pu, kissing the wonderful hands of Wio-wani, which had taught him all their skill. "Good-bye, Tiki-pu!" said Wio-wani, embracing him tenderly. "Now I am sending my second self into the world. When you are tired and want rest, come back to me: old Wio-wani will take you in."

Tiki-pu was sobbing, and the tears were running down his cheeks as he stepped out of Wio-wani's wonderfully painted garden and stood once more upon earth. Turning, he saw the old man walking away along the path toward the little door under the palace wall. At the door Wio-wani turned back and waved his hand for the last time. Tiki-pu still stood watching him. Then the door opened and shut, and Wio-wani was gone. Softly as a flower the picture seemed to have folded its leaves over him.

Tiki-pu leaned a wet face against the picture and

kissed the door in the palace wall, which Wio-wani had painted so beautifully. "O Wio-wani, dear master," he cried, "are you there?"

He waited and called again, but no voice answered him.

ELEVEN

Happy Returns

By the side of a great river, whose stream formed the boundary to two countries, lived an old ferryman and his wife. All the day, while she minded the house, he sat in his boat by the ferry, waiting to carry travelers across; or, when no travelers came, and he had his boat free, he would cast dragnets along the bed of the river for fish. But for the food, which he was able thus to procure at times, he and his wife might well have starved, for travelers were often few and far between, and often they grudged him the few pence he asked for ferrying them; and now he had grown so old and feeble that when the river was in flood he could scarcely ferry the boat across; and continually he feared lest a younger and stronger man should come and take his place and the bread from his mouth.

But he had trust in Providence. "Will not God," he said, "who has given us no happiness in this life, save in each other's help and companionship, allow us to end our days in peace?"

And his wife answered, "Yes, surely, if we trust Him enough, He will."

One morning, it being the first day of the year, the ferryman going down to his boat, found that during the night it had been loosed from its moorings and taken across the river, where it now lay fastened to the further bank.

"Wife," said he, "I can remember this same thing happening a year ago, and the year before also. Who is this traveler who comes once a year, like a thief in the night, and crosses without asking me to ferry him over?"

"Perhaps it is the good folk," said his wife. "Go over and see if they have left no coin behind them in the boat."

The old man got onto a log and poled himself across and found, down in the keel of the boat, the mark of a man's bare foot driven deep into the wood; but there was no coin or other trace to show who it might be.

Time went on; the old ferryman was all bowed down with age, and his body was racked with pains. So slow was he now in making the passage of the stream that all travelers who knew those parts took a road higher up the bank, where a stronger ferryman plied.

Winter came, and hunger and want pressed hard at the old man's door. One day while he drew his net along the stream, he felt the shock of a great fish striking against the meshes down below, and presently, as the net came in, he saw a shape like living silver, leaping and darting to and fro to find some way of escape. Up to the bank he landed it, a great gasping fish.

When he was about to kill it, he saw, to his astonishment, tears running out of its eyes that gazed at him and seemed to reproach him for his cruelty. As he drew back, the Fish said: "Why should you kill me, who wish to live?"

The old man, altogether bewildered at hearing himself thus addressed, answered: "Since I and my wife are hungry, and God gave you to be eaten, I have good reason for killing you."

"I could give you something worth far more than a meal," said the Fish, "if you would spare my life."

"We are old," said the ferryman, "and want only to end our days in peace. Today we are hungry; what can be more good for us than a meal, which will give us strength for the morrow, which is the new year?"

The Fish said: "Tonight someone will come and unfasten your boat and ferry himself over, and you know nothing of it till the morning when you see the craft moored out yonder by the further bank."

The old man remembered how the thing had happened in previous years, directly the Fish spoke. "Ah, you know that then! How is it?" he asked.

"When you go back to your hut at night to sleep,

I am here in the water," said the Fish. "I see what goes on."

"What goes on, then?" asked the old man, very curious to know who the strange traveler might be.

"Ah," said the Fish, "if you could only catch him in your boat, he could give you something you might wish for! I tell you this: do you and your wife keep watch in the boat all night, and when he comes, and you have ferried him into midstream, where he cannot escape, then throw your net over him and hold him till he pays you for all your ferryings."

"How shall he pay me? All my ferryings of a lifetime!

"Make him take you to the land of Returning Time. There, at least, you can end your days in peace."

The old man said: "You have told me a strange thing; and since I mean to act on it, I suppose I must let you go. If you have deceived me, I trust you may yet die a cruel death."

The Fish answered: "Do as I tell you, and you shall die a happy one." And, saying this, he slipped down into the water and disappeared.

The ferryman went back to his wife supperless and said to her: "Wife, bring a net and come down into the boat!" And he told her the story of the Fish and of the yearly traveler.

They sat long together under the dark bank, looking out over the quiet and cold moonlit waters, till the midnight hour. The air was chill, and to keep them-

selves warm they covered themselves over with the net and lay down in the bottom of the boat. It was the very hour when the old year dies and the new year is born.

Before they well knew that they had been asleep, they started to feel the rocking of the boat, and found themselves out upon the broad waters of the river. And there in the forepart of the boat, clear and sparkling in the moonlight, stood a naked man of shining silver. He was bending upon the pole of the boat, and his long hair fell over it right down into the water.

The old couple rose up quietly, and unwinding themselves from the net, threw it over the Silver Man, over his head and hands and feet, and dragged him down into the bottom of the boat.

The old man caught the ferry pole and heaved the boat still into the middle of the stream. As he did so, a gentle shock came to the heart of each; feebly it fluttered and sank low. "Oh, wife!" sighed the old man, and reached out his hand for hers.

The Silver Man lay still in the folds of the net and looked at them with a wise and quiet gaze. "What would you have of me?" he said, and his voice was far off and low.

They said, "Bring us into the land of Returning Time."

The Silver Man said: "Only once can you go there, and once return."

They both answered, "We wish once to go there, and once return."

So he promised them that they should have the whole of their request; and they unloosed him from the net and landed altogether on the further bank.

Up the hill they went, following the track of the Silver Man. Presently they reached its crest; and there before them lay all the howling winter of the world.

The Silver Man turned his face and looked back; and looking back, it became all young and ruddy and bright. The ferryman and his wife gazed at him, both speechless at the wonderful change. He took their hands, making them turn the way by which they had come; below their feet was a deep black gulf, and beyond and away lay nothing but a dark, starless hollow of air.

"Now," said their guide, "you have but to step forward one step, and you shall be in the land of Returning Time."

They loosed hold of his hands, joined clasp, husband with wife, and at one step upon what seemed gulf beneath their feet, found themselves in a green and flowery land. There were perfumed valleys and grassy hills, whose crops stretched down before the breeze; thick fleecy clouds crossed their tops, and overhead amid a blue air rang the shrill trilling of birds. Behind lay, fading mistily as a dream, the bare world they had left; and fast on his forward road, growing small to them from a distance, went the Silver Man, a shining point on the horizon.

The ferryman and his wife looked and saw youth in each other's faces beginning to peep out through the furrows of age; each step they took made them

grow younger and stronger; years fell from them like
worn-out rags as they went down into the valleys of the
land of Returning Time.

How fast Time returned! Each step made the change
of a day, and every mile brought them five years back
toward youth. When they came down to the streams that
ran in the bed of each valley, the ferryman and his wife
felt their prime return to them. He saw the gold come
back into her locks, and she the brown into his. Their
lips became open to laughter and song. "Oh, how good,"
they cried, "to have lived all our lives poor, to come at
last to this!"

They drank water out of the streams and tasted the
fruit from the trees that grew over them; till presently,
being tired for mere joy, they lay down in the grass to
rest. They slept hand within hand and cheek against
cheek and, when they woke, found themselves quite
young again, just at the age when they were first
married in the years gone by.

The ferryman started up and felt the desire of life
strong in his blood. "Come!" he said to his wife, "or
we shall become too young with lingering here. Now
we have regained our youth, let us go back into the
world once more!"

His wife hung upon his hand, "Are we not happy
enough," she asked, "as it is? Why should we return?"

"But," he cried, "we shall grow too young; now
we have youth and life at its best, let us return! Time
goes too fast with us; we are in danger of it carrying
us away."

She said no further word but followed up toward the way by which they had entered. And yet, in spite of her wish to remain, as she went, her young blood frisked. Presently coming to the top of a hill, they set off running and racing; at the bottom they looked at each other and saw themselves boy and girl once more.

"We have stayed here too long!" said the ferryman, and pressed on.

"Oh, the birds," sighed she, "and the flowers and the grassy hills to run on, we are leaving behind!" But still the boy had the wish for a man's life again and urged her on; and still with every step they grew younger and younger. At length, two small children, they came to the border of that enchanted land and saw beyond the world, bleak and wintry and without leaf. Only a further step was wanted to bring them face to face once more with the hard battle of life.

Tears rose in the child-wife's eyes: "If we go," she said, "we can never return!" Her husband looked long at her wistful face; he, too, was more of a child now and was forgetting his wish to be a man again.

He took hold of her hand and turned around with her, and together they faced once more the flowery orchards and the happy watered valleys.

Away down there light streams tinkled and birds called. Downward they went, slowly at first, then with dancing feet, as with shoutings and laughter they ran.

Down into the level fields they ran; their running was turned to a toddling; their toddling to a tumbling; their tumbling to a slow crawl upon hands and feet

among the high grass and flowers; till at last they were lying side by side, curled up into a cuddly ball, chuckling and dimpling and crowing to the insects and birds that passed over them.

Then they heard the sweet laughter of Father Time; and over the hill he came, young, ruddy, and shining, and gathered them up sound asleep on the old boat by the ferry.

TWELVE

Knoonie in the Sleeping Palace

Just when the palace fell into its deep sleep, the porter's son had run out to follow a swarm of bees, which had flown over the fish ponds into the woods lying outside the royal demesne. In the very minute after he had climbed the wood pales, to the time when the shifty swarm came swinging its long bright tangle for home, calling on him to retrace his pursuit, sleep had clapped down like a great eyelid over the whole palace.

Knoonie made a clear leap over the palings into the royal clover; and then felt something hurting his heart, he could not know what or why, very strange, very frightening; it was like waking up all alone in the middle of a dark night and feeling that something was standing quite still in the silence before him—quite

still, because he himself had moved. He took one step forward and at that sprang aside as if a snake were under him: his foot had made no sound in the clover! Then, thinking his ears must have deceived him, he tried once more. Ah! now it was so frightful that his courage went utterly: "Help, help!" he cried with all the force of his lungs: but his voice gave no sound. The dead silence that weighed on his struggles to cry drove him wild with terror.

He set off running as if Death were after him: running like a blind thing; and knew nothing more till he fell half-stunned and bleeding into the gateway of the palace courtyard.

He sprang and tapped with his hand on the porter's wicket. "Father, dear father, open quick!" he cried. But the words fell mute, and the wicket did not open. Then he began beating with his fists on the bronze panels and, seizing hold of the knocker, battered for dear life. For dear life! But dear reason almost died in the attempt. The great bronze knocker beat without making a sound. He stopped his ears with his fingers to get rid of the stillness, which was so terrible: and then at last he began to think that while in the wood he must have gone stone-deaf. But he was frightened; though he was deaf, others surely should hear him: again he beat and beat upon the knocker, throwing his whole weight upon it, and cried with the tears running down his face for his father to come to him.

Surely somebody must come. No, all was quite still as well as silent: nothing moved: everywhere it was

the same. There was a sentry on guard over the gate: Knoonie could see his helmet and the top of his halbert shining in the sun. He cried to him to come down and let him in; but the man stood so still that he began to think he must truly have lost the power of speech as well as of hearing. He stooped down, and taking up a stone, threw it at the soldier to make him turn around; moving away from the wall so as to get a better aim, he was able to see more of him. The sentry stood very strangely; he must be asleep or sunstruck, for a small green parrakeet had come and perched on his shoulder.

The fifth stone Knoonie threw (for fear had made his hand tremble) hit the soldier on the head; and yet he did not wake up, and the strange little parrakeet remained as if stuffed and glued to its perch.

Then Knoonie, casting his eyes all round for anything to help, saw a new sight. All down the broad avenues of the park a movement was taking place from the earth upward: it came nearer and nearer: it was like a green army on the march: it waved long prickly spears and many-pointed crests and sent green things like lizards swarming into the high trees that stood in its way. Up and up, closer and higher to the very gates of the palace it came—a wall of thistles, magic in strength and stature, overranked by beetling heads of hemlock and underrun by long snakey loops of bramble that writhed in and out of the earth like huge worms.

"I must be dreaming!" thought Knoonie for a way out of his distress. "It's all one horrid dream, which will come to an end just as the worst thing happens."

But the giant thistles came crowding close, reaching hungry hands at him. He caught hold of the knocker and, dragging himself up, was able in his terror to force open the wicket and work his small body through, just as the first thistle caught him by the leg. He escaped shoeless and with all his hose torn into ribbons from the knee. Inside he came upon his father, sitting in his accustomed niche, keys in hand, sitting quite still with head bent and closed eyes.

The child began to tremble and cry; he forgot any longer to think it was a dream; a remembrance like the touch of dead lips chilled his heart: the remembrance that while his father had been sitting there almost within reach of his hand, he, Knoonie, had cried and beaten with all his force upon the door and had not been heard. He threw his arms round his father's neck, and clinging close to the deaf face he loved: "Father, father," he cried, "wake!" But his words had no sound, and the porter made no sound or stir.

Dead, dead! Knoonie threw up his hands and, trying vainly to utter one call for help, darted into the palace.

After a long time, he came out again with a white face, looking dazed into the sunlight: what was it he had seen in there? Beautiful lords and ladies, still as death, smiling and bending over golden plates and half-tasted wine; serving men who stood upright and still as death, carrying dishes and tilting out the wine into great tankards; and, over all, the yellow sunlight streaming in licked the dead faces as a beast licks carrion.

He ran tottering over the marble pavement, as fast as fear would send him; to get away out of the palace and fetch help for all these dead or dying people: for there must still be somebody left somewhere. But when he came to the porter's lodge, there was a sight in the wicket that stopped him: the small square aperture was bulged through by thistle and bramble, in the midst of which his little shoe hung trussed and skewered; the hard grasp of the thistles had bent it out of shape, and the thorns of the bramble had cut into the leather like the steel teeth of a trap. Looking through, he could see nothing but one dense forest of thistles, made the more impassable by a thick mesh of creepers that clung about their stems. He climbed up on to the walls: everywhere was the same; those death's heads of hemlock had grown higher than the trees of the park and threw their shadows over the whole palace.

Slowly, the meaning of the horror, which had first been so impossible for his mind to take in, grew clear to his imagination. The sleeping palace—that whispered tale of his childhood—was embodied before him; and of all those who had heard it told and laughed it lightly away because every day brought sameness of life to each sense, he alone was left awake to drink the full cup of this sleep of doom; he alone, amid others unconscious of their arrested life, with all the ways of knowledge closed from him by an overwhelming silence, he and he only must live and move and endure this living tomb, till the Prince Rescuer should come, of whom the same tale gave promise. The great palace where

he had been such a little thing at everybody's beck and call, one for the grooms to tease and for maids and serving men to harry, was his own possession now, to do in what he would; but no joy came to him with this growing sense of a strange liberty. He went from place to place, tiptoeing at first, hardly daring to enter those grand chambers where the king and his great lords were sitting in state; but the lords-in-waiting stood making way for him with closed eyes; and he might see and touch and taste whatever he chose.

He went and stood behind great ladies and stroked their shining hair and touched their white wondrous throats and the strong hands of the knights, the King's even, with its gold signet ring; but there was no joy in any of these things. And when hunger came on him, he put out his hand and helped himself from the King's plate: yet though he had tasted no such delicacies in his life before, they gave him no pleasure now. He looked at all the beautiful ladies with their sweet-smiling lips and remembered how he had thought that to be kissed by them would be almost death, so great must be the delight. Now he climbed up to the sweetest of them all and tried to imagine her as the mother he had never known; yet when he kissed and saw how the lips went smiling on, it was such bitterness that the tears burst from his eyes and fell into the velvet lap of her dress. He caught up a napkin, "For when she wakes up she will see what a mess I have made and be angry," he thought: then he remembered the hundred years and cried still more.

At last, when it began to get dark, weary with sorrow and drawn thither by a growing fear of his loneliness, he went back to the gate, and there, kissing him, lay down with his head on his father's knee and, clinging to the hand that had hold of the keys of his prison, wept himself to sleep. Ah! how happy would he be if sleep would join his lot to theirs and his eyes never open again till the whole day of deliverance was come. Alas! That the bees should have led him beyond reach of the charm, which would have brought sleep, and only back to be enclosed in the impenetrable embrace of that thorny fastness.

The next day's sun shone down and opened Knoonie's eyes; and he rose up into the lifelong silence that encompassed him; and, kissing his father's face, went forth into the joyless splendors of his prison house.

This day he climbed all the towers and strained his eyes for a glimpse of the great unsleeping world beyond. But high and far the forest of thorns had stretched itself; and he could only see here and there the blue of the most distant hills through gaps of thicket.

Then he went down and sought out all his old acquaintances, the stableboys who played with him, the grooms who bullied, and the maids who teased. He came face to face with the terrible head cook, who had so many times threatened to beat him to a jelly; now Knoonie could have boxed the tyrant's head off, and no hand would be there to stay him; but he only stood and

looked at the big grim face and the closed eyes and longed hungrily for a blow from that coarse red fist.

He went on to the stables; and now who was there to forbid him his heart's desire to climb onto the back of the King's great charger, who stood sleeping with beautifully arched neck: yet when he had clambered his way up by the manger, it was no pride to him to be there: he only bowed his face down into the black mane and wept.

That same day he found the Princess sleeping in her chamber; oh! so beautiful she was with her little white hand laid on the spinning wheel, a small prick of scarlet showing on the delicate skin. So beautiful she was, he dared not kiss her yet, for he did not know that anyone who could win entrance into the sleeping palace, could by kissing the Princess break the charm and gain her for his bride. Already more than one brave knight had entered that vast forest of thorns and thrown away his life in striving to get to those lips, which were Knoonie's for a little stooping. But he was a child, and he did not understand.

The days went by, the weeks went by, and the child fell in with ever-deepening sadness to the loneliness of his environment. His wistful face grew beautiful and pure in that still air, and the picture of courtly life that encircled him lent him an unconscious grace. Yet he stayed humble and sad, and every night, leaving beds of down and pillows of lace untouched, went back to kiss his father's face and lie with his head on his knee. As for food, that great palace held stores, which would

suffice him through many lives; and during the magic
sleep nothing changed or decayed: even the milk stayed
fresh through the many years to come; a hundred
shining pails of it standing in the king's dairy.

The weeks, the months, even the years went by;
but the child forgot the passing of time; and the less and
less of a child, retained the child's heart still, lonely
and sad; with a child's will and brain, with the memory
of its childish prattle dying away, and no words or
thoughts of a growing man to take its place; and amid
that sleep of dreamless men, where even the thought of
evil did not enter, his heart was left to him, gentle,
simple, and pure.

Every night at his father's knee, Knoonie knelt
and said his evening prayer and slept well with the
porter's hand in his. Years made his body fair and
of a slender strength, and through the deep silence he
grew tall. And he would go and look at the sweet-faced
women and wonder why he sighed, and why it was so
sad to kiss their lips that smiled and yet cared nothing
—so sad that as years went on he left off from that
which seemed to put a double silence on his life, the
pain being too keen for his heart. And then he would
go and look at the Princess whose lips he had never
kissed: and that seemed the saddest thing of all.

Still years went on, and his mild mute life bore
him very slowly on to age: and still night by night,
a young man once, and then a man in his full prime,
and then a man with gray hair showing on his head,
and then a man beginning to bend down with age, went

and said his childish prayer and kissed his father's face and slept with his head against his father's knee.

Very gently had life cradled him to age when a hundred years came around: he had lost all knowledge or thought of speech, save that one form of daily use, and his silver-gray face was a reflection of the spirit that brooded over the sleeping palace.

The great day came when all the palace clocks and the sounds of speech and laughter woke back to life. The thorns and thistles had disappeared, dropping a child's shoe for luck over the palace threshold: the Prince had come and broken the spell. The cook was screaming that a hundred cats had been at the cream.

In a far-off corner of the palace Knoonie heard and knew what these sounds meant, and his heart trembled for joy: but it was so very terrible! To him the pain, the bewilderment, the multitude of sights and sounds made this renewed life an agony past knowing; he was so giddy he could only creep hand over hand along the wall toward the gate where his father sat. Now his one thought was to see his father.

As he came under the archway, the porter took him by the shoulder roughly and turned him out of doors. "We want no naked old beggars here."

Knoonie found no words to say; he just walked on and on, a beautiful, bowed-down old man, spoken of none, until one night he knocked at a doorway in fairyland, and there with me found contentment and a home.

Afterword

Laurence Housman, younger brother of the poet A. E. Housman, was born on July 18, 1865, at Bromsgrove, Worcestershire, England. His recollection of childhood was vivid. On the whole it was for him a happy, satisfying experience. The family was comfortably well off, though not wealthy. Laurence, his four brothers, and two sisters were allowed considerable freedom from adult supervision.

When Laurence was about five years old, his mother died. Two years later his father married his wife's favorite cousin to whom Laurence himself had proposed at the age of six! His stepmother instituted daily reading aloud, which formed a bond between the older and younger members of the family. About this time the children began to act out plays—"generally of our own composing, unwritten and impromptu." Alfred, the

eldest, was always the leader in these semi-literary activities. At first they were group undertakings, each child responsible for a character or act, but in time the children began to write separately. The last combined venture was a play, *The Tragedy of Lady Jane Grey*, for which twelve-year-old Laurence wrote the first act. Nearly twenty-five years were to pass before he would again make any serious attempt at playwriting. His father and stepmother, afraid he might wish to become an actor, discouraged visits to the theater, but performances by traveling companies made a lasting impression.

Unlike Alfred, Laurence did not excel in the classical curriculum offered at school. When it became apparent that he would never be able to earn a living in scholarly pursuits, it was decided, on the basis of his interest in drawing, that he had in him the makings of an artist. With his sister Clemence he attended the Royal College of Art in London and began illustrating short pieces and poems, his own and the work of other writers. At the age of thirty he became art critic for the *Manchester Guardian*. This gave him "confidence and a power of ready writing," and he realized that he was more naturally cut out to be an author than an artist.

Of his early authorship, he wrote, "My whole bent, as a writer, lay in the direction of fancy, fairy tale and legend." It was during this early period that he wrote most of the stories included in this collection.

Housman called himself a romantic humanist. Born into a politically conservative family (his father was a

fervid Tory), he later broke away from the narrow conservatism of his upbringing and became a feminist, a suffragist, and after World War I, a pacifist. Once his social conscience developed, drama and political satire became his main literary interests. To him, drama was the best possible medium for portraying human nature in its infinite variety: "The good and the bad, the wise and the foolish, the noble and the ridiculous." He invented the play-cycle, chapters of dramatic biography with one character as the main subject.

Laurence Housman has the distinction of being England's most censored playwright. His plays were censored because they portrayed royalty and religious personages, sometimes in an unfavorable light. *Victoria Regina*, the play by which Housman is probably best known to an American audience, suffered this fate. The ban was later removed, and in 1935 *Victoria Regina* played to crowded houses at the Gate Theatre in London in celebration of King George V's Silver Jubilee. Six months later it began a long run on Broadway with Helen Hayes in the title role. Housman considered this play and his play-cycle of the life of St. Francis, *Little Plays of St. Francis*, his best works.

Housman wrote with tremendous charm. It would be hard to excel the sheer verbal beauty of his fairy tales. The writing is lyrical. The tales have a bittersweet quality—romantic, but never saccharine; poignant, relieved by touches of humor. The individual stories are hauntingly beautiful, but it is only on reading several of them one after another that the reader feels

the impact of Housman's style and philosophy. The humanist strikes out against vanity, greed, and thoughtless cruelty in such tales as "The Rat-Catcher's Daughter" and "Gammelyn, the Dressmaker."

Evidences of childhood memories may be read into the stories. In his autobiography, *The Unexpected Years* (Jonathan Cape, 1936) Housman speaks of the garden at Bromsgrove as one of the most important influences in his development. The garden was two acres of freedom "beautifully screened from the house" (and adult eyes), "protector of our liberties and a field for individual development." This garden enters into many of his stories but most noticeably in "The Wooing of the Maze," in which the beautiful Princess Rosemary, "who had all she wanted in the world but freedom," is finally liberated from swarms of unwanted suitors by the wise and loyal gardener she loves.

Some of his stories resemble the old folk tales, but in at least one, "Knoonie in the Sleeping Palace," Housman begins where the old tale left off. The child, Knoonie, left outside the palace when the spell takes effect, lives through one hundred years of loneliness waiting for the Prince to come to awaken the Sleeping Beauty. When the spell is broken, he is unrecognized and cast out as a beggar. "Knoonie found no words to say; he just walked on and on, a beautiful bowed-down old man, spoken of none, until one night he knocked at a doorway in fairyland, and there with me found contentment and a home."

Laurence Housman died in 1959 at the age of 93.

The stories in this collection were selected from the author's out-of-print collections, *A Doorway in Fairyland* (Jonathan Cape, 1922), *Moonshine and Clover* (Jonathan Cape, 1922), *All-Fellows and the Cloak of Friendship* (Jonathan Cape, 1923), and *What O'Clock Tales* (Jonathan Cape, 1932). They were chosen for their appeal to the older reader of fairy tales and for storytellers to share in the story hour. A few, namely, "Rocking-Horse Land," "A Chinese Fairy Tale," and "The Rat-Catcher's Daughter" appeal to the younger listener and have appeared in other storytelling anthologies. Two of the tales have been recorded. Ruth Sawyer tells "A Chinese Fairy Tale" on Weston Woods record, WW 702, *Ruth Sawyer Storyteller*. "Rocking-Horse Land" is told by Mary Strang on CMS label 632, *Fairy Tale Favorites, Vol. III*. They are included here because they *are* favorites, and it is hoped that their familiarity will lead the reader on to Housman's less known fairy tales. The stories in this collection will have special appeal for girls from ten or eleven on who enjoy the Martin Pippin stories of Eleanor Farjeon, Oscar Wilde's "The Nightingale and the Rose," and the old romances—"Tristan and Iseult" and "Deirdre."

Housman himself illustrated the original tales. Of this venture he writes, "Dr. Richard Garnett had given my fairy tales a welcome with higher praise than I should have given them myself, and though the illustrations were liked by few, the stories were generally

commended." For this edition Julia Noonan has made expressive pencil drawings that evoke the romantic mood of the stories with great beauty and distinction.

TITLE II-A